MY ~~AWESOME~~ POPULARITY PLAN

AWFUL

MY ~~AWESOME~~ AWFUL

POPULARITY

PLAN

{SETH RUDETSKY}

RANDOM HOUSE 🏠 NEW YORK

Text copyright © 2012 by Seth Rudetsky
Jacket art: crown image © iStockphoto.com/Samarskaya;
helmet image © iStockphoto.com/Mervana;
disco ball image © iStockphoto.com/Alexander Shirokov

All rights reserved. Published in the United States by Random House Children's Books, a division of Random House, Inc., New York.

Random House and the colophon are registered trademarks of Random House, Inc.

Visit us on the Web! www.randomhouse.com/teens

Educators and librarians, for a variety of teaching tools, visit us at www.randomhouse.com/teachers

sethrudetsky.com

Library of Congress Cataloging-in-Publication Data
Rudetsky, Seth.
My awesome/awful popularity plan / Seth Rudetsky. — 1st ed.
p. cm.
Summary: Chubby, Jewish, and gay high school sophomore Justin Goldblatt plans to become popular by the end of the year, but instead of dating the star quarterback he catches the eye of Becky, the quarterback's girlfriend, while his best friend, Spencer, stops speaking to him.
ISBN 978-0-375-86915-0 (trade) — ISBN 978-0-375-96915-7 (lib. bdg.) — ISBN 978-0-375-87324-9 (ebook)
[1. Popularity—Fiction. 2. Gays—Fiction. 3. Best friends—Fiction. 4. Friendship—Fiction. 5. High schools—Fiction. 6. Schools—Fiction. 7. Jews—Fiction.] I. Title.
PZ7.R85513My 2012 [Fic]—dc23 2011024154

Printed in the United States of America

10 9 8 7 6 5 4 3 2 1

First Edition

Random House Children's Books supports
the First Amendment and celebrates the right to read.

This book is dedicated to
Eric Myers, who convinced me to start,
Schuyler Hooke, who encouraged me to continue,
and James Wesley, who helped me to finish.

MY ~~AWESOME~~ AWFUL POPULARITY PLAN

1

TRY TO FIGURE OUT WHICH boy I have the biggest crush on. Is it Quincy Slatton, the science genius sure to win a Westinghouse Scholarship? Is it Tally Higgins, the stoner who is always seen at school, but never in class? Is it Gary Burns, the shy introvert who blushes when you say hi but comes alive in the art room?

No, it's none of them. Why should it be? There's at least a *slight* possibility that someday I could date one of them. Instead, I've made it as difficult as possible for myself to ever fulfill my dreams of love. Yes, I, Justin Goldblatt, the school loser, have a crush on the oldest chestnut in the book—the unattainable star quarterback, Chuck Jansen! How cliché is that?

FYI, that's pronounced "clee-shay." In English class today, David Chasen was reading a Guy de Maupassant story out loud and pronounced it "clysh." Everybody, including Mr. Fabry, laughed. Even though I felt bad for David, I joined in. It felt good to finally *not* be the reason the class was laughing. Usually after I speak in class, Doug Gool will cough "faggot" into his fist. He does it in such a way that the teacher doesn't hear, but everybody else does. He's been doing it for so many years at this point that he's started to vary the words that he coughs— sometimes it's *fag*, sometimes *queer*, sometimes *gay*. I guess I should applaud his creativity. Lately, he's been using various themes, depending on what the class is focusing on: We're studying Pilgrims in social studies, so he'll cough "Thou art gay" in my direction, and since we're learning the periodic table in earth science, I've gotten used to hearing a constant chant of "*fag*nesium" whenever I speak. Most annoyingly, though, recently in geometry, after I identified a shape as a "trapezoid," he coughed "*fag*ezoid" and received a round of sustained chuckles. I was outraged . . . not merely by the insult but at what passes for homophobic rhyming mockery. At least "magnesium" and "fagnesium" have the same vowel and final consonant in the first syllable, but "trapezoid" and "fagezoid" *do not rhyme*! How dare such shoddy workmanship bring down the house?

Anyhoo, I was raucously guffawing at David Chasen when, at the height of my openmouthed laughter, Doug Gool pointed his phone at me and snapped a shot.

He flashed it around. "Look at the piece of spinach in Goldblatt's teeth!"

I quickly clamped my mouth closed, but it was too late. The proof was in his iPhone. He sent it to Jeff Horner as the bell rang, and Jeff had just enough time before everyone left to forward it to his entire contact list, which included the whole class. It was the only instance when I haven't seen everyone rush out of the room. Instead, they suddenly had all the time in the world to stand around and look at their phones. The mild laughter about David Chasen's pronunciation of *cliché* was nothing compared to the belly laughs my spinach-filled teeth got. That is what my friend Spencer calls instant karma.

"I've told you before, Justin. Karma means that whatever you do, the same is done back to you." Spencer explained it to me (for the tenth time this year) in gym class later that day. He was wearing black shorts with a black Gap V-neck that, combined with his orange hair, made him look like a Halloween centerpiece. I know orange hair sounds crazy, but it's eye-catching, fall-foliage orange, not Ronald McDonald orange.

Looks-wise, we're totally different; he resembles a Midwestern farmer while I could easily be mistaken for someone applying to rabbinical school. On top of that, he's around six inches taller than me but weighs twenty-five pounds less. I don't know which I'd rather be: tall and crazily skinny like him or short and chubby in all the wrong places like yours truly. Also, I'm jealous of Spencer because when he gets older and fills out, he's going to be great-looking, with his cute face and good hair. Since I've known him, I've seen his hair automatically style itself into something hip and trendy whether he's sweaty from gym class or soaked from a sudden rain shower or refusing to put in any product in protest of the destruction of the Amazon.

I, however, spent all of seventh through ninth grades trying to straighten my hair every morning, but by third period, it would always go back to its natural curl. And I don't mean the fun, bouncy curls you want to run your fingers through. I mean tight, Brillo-pad curls like . . . well, like a Brillo pad.

Spencer and I were essentially by ourselves outdoors. We were supposed to be running track, but we weren't. We were *jalking,* which is a word we invented that means moving much slower than jogging but one iota faster than walking. That's why most of the word is from *walking,* but the *j* is thrown in because there's a *little* essence of jogging. Once in a while, Mr. Hasley would blow his whistle at us and we'd go from a jalk to a jog.

Spencer continued explaining. "You were laughing at David Chasen, so your karma was to then have people laugh at you."

I didn't want to hear the rest of the explanation, so I feigned being out of breath and waved for him to keep moving. He stopped. He considerately waited until I stopped panting to finish his lesson in why I deserved what I got.

"Sometimes it takes a while . . . ," he continued, and then took a moment to think of an example. "Like when DeeDee Gosling returned that wallet she found and months later was crowned homecoming queen even though everybody thought Tricia Hansberry was going to get it."

He was right. That crowning had to be DeeDee's good

karma. It certainly wasn't based on her twice-monthly-washed hair.

"Sometimes, however, it's immediate, or what's called *instant karma*." He stopped and pulled out his phone to show me what he meant. "Like this."

I stared at the shot of my gaping mouth that featured what looked like a whole head of spinach in my two front teeth. I spoke with detachment. "I'm glad to see your phone has such good pixelation. I can see not only the spinach but also remnants of the processed cheese used in the cafeteria's vegetarian lasagna."

He peered at the photo. "I don't think that's because my phone is so great. I think that would be pretty obvious even with half the pixelation."

Mr. Hasley blew his whistle three times to signal the end of class, giving me a break from learning more details about why my school-wide humiliation was my own fault. The other boys hit the showers, but since Spencer and I broke nary a drop of sweat, we just went to the locker room and put our school clothes back on.

I looked at myself in the mirror. Hmm . . . maybe if I cut my hair short, my natural perm wouldn't be so big. And if I ixnayed my enormous post-homework bowl of Cinnamon Toast Crunch, I could lose some of my gut. As the saying goes, "My diet starts tomorrow."

But I didn't mean that as a homily that people

mysteriously found humorous enough to reproduce on refrigerator magnets. I was serious! I'm sick of looking the way I do. Spencer appeared in the mirror behind me. His hair was a mess . . . and it looked great. While he fixed it for no reason, I waved and left the locker room quickly so none of the boys could accuse me of lingering and looking at them (which I wanted to do). Spencer joined me in the hall and told me he wanted to get a PowerBar from the vending machine before his next class. I watched him sprint toward the cafetorium. Ironically, his running after gym class was thirty times faster than his "running" during gym class.

I had the next period free and decided to go to the library. The reading area has super-plush chairs, and I wanted to snuggle down and lose myself in *A Tale of Two Cities*. I hoped the plight of Charles Darnay would help me forget my latest school-wide humiliation. I got there right after the bell rang, and luckily my favorite chair was available. I opened my Charles Dickens but couldn't concentrate. I kept thinking about the latest picture of me being texted to everyone. Was it passing through the air particles surrounding me? Why did this kind of thing keep happening to me? I closed my eyes and tried to focus on what exactly was keeping me on the bottom of the social ladder.

On the surface, this would be a perfect problem to work out with Spencer because he's so smart, but I always have to remind myself that his advice starts out helpful and then gets annoying. Especially about social issues. Yes, last year he helped me accept being gay, but two minutes later he couldn't understand why I wanted to be popular. Infuriating.

And yet, maybe there was something helpful he said that day that I've forgotten.

Hmm . . . I decided to remember back to that afternoon in the park to see if there were any nuggets of wisdom I'd let slide by me.

I had spent all of freshman year in denial of the growing feelings I was having toward boys. I absolutely didn't want to grow up to be gay. I had been called a fag ever since fifth grade, and it had always made me feel awful about myself before I even knew what it meant. Realizing that I probably was what the name meant was too much for me. By the spring, I had successfully suppressed thinking about it.

Until that afternoon in late June.

Right after our algebra final exam, I was walking home with Spencer. We were both in a good mood because we only had one more final and it was in health, which would cover such difficult topics as "Can you get pregnant from a toilet seat?" and "Is showering good?"

We were laughing as we made up new topics—"Should you set your hair on fire?" or "How many venereal diseases equal a bushel?"—when we passed by Doug Gool and his friends in front of the Ben & Jerry's. Even though the other boys in his gang tower over him, Doug is clearly the leader. He's my height (short) and weight (heavy) but it's all muscle. He's always sported his white-blond hair in a scary crew cut, and two years ago he broke his nose in a big fight with a wrestler from Woodmere Academy. His beady eyes, army haircut, off-center nose, and bulging muscles equal terrifying-looking.

"Hey, Fag Goldblatt!" Doug said as we walked by. "Laughing about faggy things?"

I sped up and Spencer followed. It was one thing to be called a fag when I was by myself, but to have a friend witness it was awful.

When we got a block away, I started talking about health class again, hoping Spencer would pretend that nothing had happened. Instead he said, "Doug Gool is a douche bag."

I tried to laugh but couldn't; I still felt so embarrassed. I wanted to say, "I hate being called a fag," but I said, "I hate being a fag."

Suddenly, complete silence. We were in front of the park, and the only noise was from the toddlers on the swing sets.

Spencer looked at me seriously. "Justin, you're not a fag." He said it firmly. He obviously wanted me to believe it. But at that point, I was sick of denying it to myself.

"Spencer, I *am* a fag."

I expected him to be disgusted. But he wasn't. He gave me the same look he had just given me. "Justin, you may be gay, but you're not a fag. *Fag* is a mean word that douche bags use to make gay people feel bad about themselves."

"What?" He was confusing me with his not caring about my announcement. I decided to reiterate it. "Spencer, listen to what I'm telling you—I like boys. I am what they say I am. I'm a fag."

"And, Justin, I'm asking you this—you're Jewish, right?" I nodded. "Does that mean you're a kike?"

Hmm . . .

I began to see what he meant. It was the first time I separated being gay from being called a fag.

He continued. "Just because we're not what the majority is doesn't mean we have to take on the a-hole-like words they attach to us."

Good point, I thought. Then, *Wait a minute!* He had said, *Just because we're not what the majority is . . .* Spencer wasn't Jewish.

I managed a weak "We?"

He stood up taller. "Yes, Justin. I like boys, too. And I'm not a fag."

OH MY GOD! My best friend was gay! Now I could discuss all the guys I'd been harboring crushes on! I began to calculate in my head . . . We needed at least two to three hours for grades six through eight and then four more hours just for ninth grade!

Suddenly a thought hit me: Spencer seemed so sure of himself. Did that mean . . .

"Spencer, you say you're gay like you've . . . you know . . . proved it."

"Proved it?" he asked. "Do you mean have I quote-unquote

been with anybody?" He laughed. "Hardly. The only boys I've been with remain in my Abercrombie and Fitch catalogs."

I knew what he was driving at and didn't want the details. Health class at least taught me it didn't cause hairy palms.

Then I got annoyed. "If we're both gay, why am *I* always the one being called a fag?"

He thought for a minute. "I don't know . . . I'm quieter than you. People don't seem to notice me. You're certainly more 'out there.'"

"Meaning what?" I asked indignantly.

"Well, you were pretty public about wanting to make the day of the Tony Award nominations a school holiday."

I was incensed. "They announce them at eight-thirty a.m. sharp! It's unfair that I have to wait until first period ends to check my phone and find out what's up for Best Musical!"

Spencer smiled and held up his hand to stop me. "You don't have to convince me, but most teenage boys don't care about Broadway. Or if they do, they don't admit it."

He had a point. Most boys in our school were obsessed with sports and not the latest Sondheim revival.

He continued. "Broadway is thought of as a girl thing, and if a boy likes it, the narrow minds in school will label him a fag."

He was on to something. "So," I reasoned, "if I start pretending I like different things, the other kids'll stop making fun of me?"

Spencer looked annoyed. "I guess . . . but why do you want to be who you're not?"

We started walking into the park. It was a gorgeous day and we loved sitting by Goose Pond and watching the rowboats.

"I don't want to be who I'm not. . . . I just want people to like me."

Spencer stopped walking. "People *do* like you."

Was he crazy? I was one of the most unpopular kids in school. The only ones less popular were the hippie guidance counselor's daughter and that ten-year-old who started high school when he was nine.

"People like me?" I asked. He nodded emphatically. I couldn't believe he was trying to make me believe a lie. "People like me?" I was getting angry. "*No one* likes me!" I yelled.

"Oh, really?" Spencer yelled back. I knew I'd pissed him off. Spencer hardly ever yells. Except at Young Republicans. "I guess I'm no one—even though I've been your friend since Mrs. Gibson's class!"

He was right. We met in fifth grade and first bonded over *The Simpsons.* We were the only boys in our class who were more obsessed with Comic Book Guy than with Bart. Yes, "Eat my shorts" is funny the first few times you hear it, but "Worst (fill-in-the-blank) ever" is always hilarious.

"Spencer," I said, calming down. "I know you're my friend and I appreciate it, but you just don't know what it's like to have everybody—*mostly* everybody—dislike you."

We had walked all the way to the pond. It was one of those global-warming super-sunny days, so we sat on a bench with a huge tree shading it.

"Maybe I don't have people actively dislike me like they dislike you, but you never even try to make friends."

That was a lie! "Yes, I do! I'd love to hang out with the Michelle Edelton group or Ty and his eleventh-grade friends."

"Exactly!" Spencer said, pointing at me. "You only want to be friends with the super-popular kids, whether or not they're dicks. You're never friendly to any of my friends."

Ouch. He was right. But Spencer was friends with kids who were one echelon—or *maybe* one and a half—above me. And once he even ate lunch with that ten-year-old. "I talk to your friends at lunch," I offered, trying to appear nice.

He let out a laugh. "You only talk to them because you have no choice—they're sitting right next to you."

I tried not to look like he was totally right.

"Justin, I can tell you'd cut the conversation off in a minute if a popular kid started talking to you."

"What's wrong with wanting to be popular?" I asked.

"That's not why you make friends." Spencer was talking to me like he was my dad. It was annoying. "The kids you're chasing after don't share any of your interests. Do you really want to sit around discussing whether Michelle Edelton should or shouldn't get a nose job for her Sweet Sixteen?"

Not really. Especially since there was nothing to debate. She *should* get a nose job . . . preferably by her Sweet Fifteen.

"By the way," he said quietly, "I'm sorry I didn't say anything when Gool called you a fag."

"Don't worry," I said. "No one wants to get beat up by him for talking back."

He seemed surprised. "Oh, I'm not scared of getting beat up. I'm just trying to practice a Zen thing of not responding to negative energy."

Oy! Lately he was doing nonstop name-dropping of various Dr. Phil/psychobabble/Eastern religion theories. Unfortunately, I asked him to clarify.

"Well," he explained, "I'm basing it on the theory that if a tree falls in the forest and nobody hears it, it hasn't fallen. In other words, if I don't respond to negative energy, it doesn't exist."

I was still trying to understand the tree-falling-silently theory when my cell phone rang.

It was my mom reminding me I had a violin lesson in an hour.

I hung up and turned back to Spencer. "Look, I have to go home, but I appreciate everything you've said today." Even though I didn't understand half of it and disagreed with more than 30 percent.

"Justin," he said as he left, "you don't have to be somebody you're not."

Hmph. *That's easy for him to say,* I thought as I walked home. Everybody likes him. Or at least ignores him.

I snapped out of my remembrance as my *Tale of Two Cities*

slipped to the floor. I picked it up. I knew I should finish the chapter since we were going to be tested on it, but I suddenly didn't care if I got an A or an F on the exam. People would still ignore me in the hallways. Besides, there was only around ten minutes left until the bell rang. That's right—it took me almost an entire period to think through what happened that afternoon, and it had been a big waste of my time. Spencer hadn't said anything helpful to get me out of the loser bin. His main advice was "be yourself." But I don't *want* to be myself if the rest of my high school years are going to be like this morning. I want more. Why should I settle for being so near the lowest rung of the school's popularity ladder? And even though there's not much further to go, every day I keep getting lower and lower. It's only three weeks into sophomore year and I've already dropped two rungs.

I recently did an informal calculation and figured out that 94 percent of freshmen are more popular than me! I thought that everybody hated freshmen. That's supposed to be the fun of being an upperclassman. Somehow I've become the exception to the age-old rule. My loserishness has trumped the inherent loserishness of almost the entire freshman class— even that kid who carries around his tuba!

I sat in the library and finally gave thought to something that's secretly dwelled in the back of my mind for years.

I'll always be a loser.

Then I said it out loud. "I'll always be a loser."

It made me feel terrible.

But . . . there was something familiar about that sentence. Who did it sound like?

My mom!

"I'll always be a college dropout." My mom has said that my whole life whenever people would ask her what she did for a living. Well, she wouldn't say that right away. First, she would look at me as if she were thinking, *Should I say this in front of him?* and then she'd plunge right in with the backstory. "Well, I had *planned* on having a career, but suddenly there I was . . . twenty and pregnant. . . ." She'd shake her head and trail off. My mom and dad met in college and, according to them, fell in love and got married their junior year. I say "according to them" because my grandmother let slip one Seder after too much Passover wine that the main reason they got married was so they could live in off-campus housing. Regardless, after a few months, my mom got pregnant with me and quit school to have me. By the time she felt I was old enough for her to go back to school, it was too late. She couldn't bear to be the one older person sitting in the classroom with twenty-year-olds. "I remember taking sociology with a sixty-year-old woman who'd suddenly decided to go back to school," she'd say. "I didn't want that to be me. Everyone in the class called her Wrinkleface."

My father would always interrupt. "But her last name was *Winkle*face! She deserved it."

"That's not the point," she'd say, and then sigh as she ended with her classic line: "I'll always be a college dropout." She would follow that statement with what could pass as a laugh if you based it on sound alone, but when you factored in her face, you'd know it was actually sadness and regret escaping her mouth with sound attached.

Except now everything was different.

A few months ago, she saw one of those women-talking-about-women's-stuff TV shows and asked me how to use the "World Wide Web." Soon, she bought her own laptop and started "Goo-gul-ing" (she drives me crazy by always pronouncing it with three syllables), and now she's online every day, taking college courses.

However, she's only taking two classes a semester, so she keeps telling me that she probably won't graduate college until I do, but "at least I won't be a college dropout anymore."

Even though it's annoying to constantly have her asking me to explain "new math," it's pretty amazing that she's changed what she thought could never change.

Wait a minute . . . if she can do it, I can do it, can't I?

YES!

And I don't want to wait until I'm in my midthirties to get myself together like she did. I'm starting NOW!

Hmm . . . there's no online course for unbecoming the school loser, so apparently I'll have to make it up myself.

OK, I'm writing this down so it's official:

I, Justin Goldblatt, will, by the end of sophomore year:

a. start dating someone. (PLEASE let it be Chuck.)
b. have my first kiss.
c. become popular.

I don't think this list is totally impossible. Other kids go out on dates and get kissed. Why can't I? *Give me one reason!* Besides the Jewfro and thirty-five-inch waist. There must be someone out there who'd find that attractive (hopefully Chuck). And as for becoming popular, it could happen. Granted, I have to somehow magically overcome being disliked by basically an entire school, but I have the whole year to do it. There are 1,300 kids in the school, so . . . if I divide that by 180 days, which is the typical school year, minus the three weeks I've already lost . . . hmm . . . OK, I have to make 8.3 kids a day not hate me. "Not hate me"? Why am I thinking small? How about worship me?! And what's with 8.3 kids a day? Let me challenge myself by bringing it up to 8.6!

Excellent. Now I have a plan.

Actually, looking over this piece of paper, it seems I more have a list of the results I want *without* the actual plan. Well, at least I'm about to see my football-playing, soon-to-be (possible) boyfriend in French class. Maybe gazing at his gorgeous-ity will trigger something in me besides the usual excessive sweating. Wish me luck!

AS I RAN TO CLASS, I realized I had forgotten my French notebook, so I had to double back to my locker. I ran past the library and as I entered the hallway with my locker, I saw Mrs. Cortale, the guidance counselor, sitting at her desk. She was eating a bowl of something that was eight different shades of green. I'm a vegetarian but she goes many steps further than me by being a raw vegan. That means she'll pretty much only eat what most people would consider a lovely corsage. She's the school's resident hippie, and her daughter, Mary Ann, is being raised like one, too. Apparently Mary Ann is forbidden to shave any hair on her body, just like her mom. Unfortunately, while it's not noticeable on the very fair-haired Mrs. Cortale (née Olsen), Mary Ann's father is Italian. You do the math. Actually, I will: two plus two equals a full head of black hair under each arm. Plus, her mother believes in "living simple in every aspect," so Mary Ann's wardrobe consists only of two non-animal/organic/environmentally friendly, shapeless sack dresses that flow down to the tips of her all-season Birkenstocks. Suffice it to say, she is equal to me in popularity, and typical of my luck, her locker is next to mine. That means that whenever someone writes something mean on her locker, they always add something to mine because the proximity makes it so deliciously easy. The reason I know they write on hers first is because I often arrive to find YOU SUCK or LOSER scrawled across her locker with mine sporting a YOU TOO or LOSER NUMBER TWO. The weird times are when she gets there before I do and wipes her locker off, so I arrive to see a cryptic SO DO YOU scrawled on mine and have no point of reference to be insulted by.

Anyway, I got to my locker and found packages of dental floss taped all over it. Obviously a reference to the spinach incident but quite frankly something I could always use. Finally, I thought, some vandalism that could be repurposed.

I placed the dental floss on the top shelf of my locker, silently cursing that it was plain and not mint flavored. Cheap asses. I walked into Monsieur Bissel's class right as the second bell was ringing and plopped down in front of Doug Gool. Oh yeah. That's one of the "great" things about my school district. We always sit alphabetically and, because my last name is Goldblatt, I get to always be in incredibly close proximity to Doug, which would be excellent if weight loss could be achieved from fear-based high blood pressure.

The only advantage to the alphabetical seating is that I sit diagonally across from Chuck Jansen, my soon-to-be-possibly-one-day quarterback boyfriend. Every day I have an excellent view of his profile (perfect, with a strong nose, pouting mouth, sexily stubbled chin, piercing blue eyes) and often get to see him run his hands through his sandy blond hair, which he boldly has grown longer than the other guys at school. It's not crazily long (I've never been into that hippie look), ending around an inch and a half below his ears.

Of course, I'm just estimating that it's an inch and half below . . . who knows?

All right, I admit that I spent hours analyzing his yearbook photo from last year and getting his exact hair dimensions by using basic calculus and a protractor. Sue me.

Anyway, Monsieur Bissel began class by teaching us an idiom that meant something like "I feel hungry and thirsty, but if I had to choose, definitely more thirsty than hungry." I thought, *When the hell am I ever going to use that in a French conversation?* It's never been something necessary to clarify in English and I've spoken that for the last fifteen years of my life.

Suddenly I heard Chuck laugh and whisper to Becky, his ex-girlfriend, "When the hell am I ever going to use that in a French conversation?"

Gasp! It's a sign! What are the odds that he would use the exact wording of my thought if we weren't meant to be together?

Becky giggled and then Chuck laughed louder, and suddenly Monsieur Bissel looked up from his Big Book of Idioms and glared in their direction.

"Chuck?" said Mr. Bissel. "Would you care to tell *la classe* why I just heard a big *rire* from your *bouche*?"

Monsieur Bissel always spoke to us with a crazy version of half English and half French. FYI, *rire* is pronounced "reer" and it means "laugh," and *bouche*, pronounced "boosh," means "mouth."

Chuck looked up innocently and said, "Gee, Monsieur Bissel, I don't know why my *rire* is so big." In case the class didn't get the reference to his rear end, he decided to push it further. "To be honest, my *rire* has always been big, but most people who've seen my *bouche* know that it's even bigger!" His pronunciation of *bouche* sounded much more like "bush," and that's all it took for the room to be filled with *rire*ing.

"*C'est tout!*" Monsieur Bissel slammed his idiom book closed. "Chuck! Detention *après* school!"

"But he has football practice!" Becky blurted out.

"Not today, he doesn't," Monsieur Bissel said curtly. "And for speaking *sans* raising your *main*, Mademoiselle Becky, you'll be in detention as well!"

Chuck and Becky looked annoyed, but this gave me an idea. I'd never actually spoken to Chuck before but perhaps I could today. He'd be in detention without his moron sidekicks for a full hour. If I could hang out in that room, maybe I could at least become friends with him, if not ask him out. I know it's crazy to think that he would ever date me, or even that he might be gay, but I've decided that sophomore year is the year I'm gonna dream big and go for what I want.

Hmm, I thought, *how can I get into detention?* I'd already handed in my homework at the beginning of class, so that eliminated the possibility of being punished for not having it. I decided to pull the old talking-without-raising-my-hand routine.

"What's the homework today?" I asked loudly while Monsieur was talking. I figured interrupting him would be sure to get his dander up. Instead, he chuckled. "My, it's nice to see such dedication from *un etudiant.*" He looked sternly at the other kids. "Would that more of you were like Justin." He smiled kindly in my direction. "It's chapter *quatre* in your *livre.*"

Rats! That didn't work. I'd have to push it. But how? While he started describing the pluperfect, Chuck began quietly rapping. "Hey, Bissel, ring the bell for dismissal."

Chuck would do this all the time and pass it down the row. The unspoken rule was that when it got to you, you'd have to repeat the rap you just heard and then make up a new one. The trick, though, was to do it quietly enough so Monsieur didn't hear but loud enough so the other kids could.

Roger Stanton, who fancied himself a soon-to-be rap star, was next. "Hey, Bissel, ring the bell for dismissal," he repeated, and added some fancy moves. Then, "Hey, Bissel, this class has no sizzle!"

Monsieur Bissel kept conjugating obliviously, and now Doug Gool was up. "Hey, Bissel, this class has no sizzle. Hey, Bissel, I gotta take a whiz-zle!"

It was my turn. I *had* to get that detention. I decided it was now or never. "Hey, Bissel, I gotta take a whiz-zle!" I rapped, full voice, hoping to get busted. But right at that moment, Monsieur had a coughing fit and didn't hear. I had to raise the volume on my new rap. Uh-oh! I hadn't thought of one. I panicked and yelled the first rhyme that came to my head.

"Hey, Bissel, how about a kiss-el?!?!"

Total silence.

Followed by class-wide laughter. As opposed to the Chuck laughter, these guffaws were not in alliance *with* me, but aimed with derision *at* me. They were literally accompanied by finger pointing, just like in a Peanuts cartoon.

Monsieur Bissel turned red.

"*Fermez les bouches!*" he bellowed. "Justin! You will be joining Chuck and Becky in detention."

Yes! Mission accomplished!

"And, class, since you find Justin so *très drôle . . .*"

Uh-oh.

". . . I want you all to think about him as you write your extra assignment for *ce soir.* A two-hundred-word essay on Paris."

The bell rang. Doug Gool stood in my way as I got up. "Thanks, dickhead. Because of you, we have to waste our night writing about Gay Paree."

I tried to move around him. He blocked me. "Hey, every-one!" he yelled. "Don't forget to do the essay, 'Justin's Gay

Paree.'" He started repeating it in rhythm. "Justin's Gay Paree! Justin's Gay Paree!"

Everyone started chanting it with Doug leading a parade out of the room. That gave me a chance to scurry around them and avoid the glowering of Monsieur Bissel.

Well, at least I got everyone's mind off the spinach incident. *And* I'm one step closer to snagging Chuck. This kind of thinking is what Spencer calls looking at the glass as half full. He said the difference between an optimist and a pessimist is that an optimist sees a glass half filled with water and calls it half full while a pessimist sees the same glass and calls it half empty.

I got to my locker. Someone had broken the lock. I looked inside. *Hmm,* I pondered, *what does an optimist call a locker half filled with bags of spinach?*

I ARRIVED IN DETENTION ONE minute before the bell rang. There's a fifteen-minute free period before all after-school activities began and I spent it in the bathroom. Not because of an upset stomach, but because I had just gotten some toothpaste with whitener and realized that I didn't have time to wait for the results of brushing three times a day for a month. This was an emergency! I needed blindingly white teeth to impress Chuck by 3:15, so I spent a full ten minutes brushing my chompers. Unfortunately, any white that might have been added to my teeth was overshadowed by the red of my bleeding gums. I don't normally have the gums of a seventy-year-old smoker, but I think the vigorous stroking of my newly bought "firm" toothbrush caused some capillary damage. I thankfully remembered learning in earth science that cold makes things contract, so I swished some cold water in my mouth frantically for the last two minutes and my gums called a truce.

I ran into the detention room (which during the day is the computer room) and saw that the teacher du jour was "E.R." E.R. is actually Ms. Horvath, the head of the English department *and* the biggest hypochondriac east of the Mississip'. Spencer and I nicknamed her E.R. because she always seems on the verge of being sent to the emergency room. Hmm . . . I guess we came up with the nickname before his obsession with karma.

Although she always acts put out by her weekly phantom maladies, she obviously enjoys each one because her normal depressed personality seems to come alive only when talking about them. I'm used to seeing her with her arm in a sling gesticulating wildly to some fellow teacher and grimacing about her "bum fibula" or scurrying to her acupuncture session while loudly proclaiming to random passersby, "Those painful needles are simply not helping my colon do its job regularly." I dreaded what today's physical duress would be. As soon as I walked in, she waved me frantically over to her desk. I approached warily, and she promptly handed me a preprinted 5 x 7 card from a stack she had next to her. I read it quickly:

> I have LOST MY VOICE. My doctor thinks it will return if I'm on <u>complete</u> vocal rest. Also, my sciatica is flaring up so I am not able to leave this chair without EXTREME pain to my lower back.

I nodded sympathetically and muttered, "Sorry." She started to say "Thank you," but all I heard was a raspy version of the word *thank* that was quickly cut off by a dramatic coughing fit, interrupted only by her looking up to see if I was taking in her star turn. She finished with a noisy spit into a tissue, and then quickly wrote something on a pad, which she handed to me.

It HURTS!

I didn't quite know if she meant her voice or the sciatica but found no need to ask since she was one step ahead of me and answered my unasked question by jabbing her fingers simultaneously at her throat and lower back. Thankfully, the bell rang and I told her to feel better and turned around to zero in on my prey. Score! Chuck was sitting in the back of the room, and even though Becky was across from him, the seat behind him was blissfully empty! I started to walk down the row when I locked eyes with the only other detentionee: Pamela Austin. She was in her signature matching skirt and sweater ensemble with a piano-key scarf wrapped casually around her neck. Pamela had a pretty face but it was overshadowed by her "I haven't had a haircut since I was six" hair that hung straight down her back. I suddenly did a double take: Pamela was such a Goody Two-shoes. . . . Why the hell was she here? She must have seen the quizzical expression in my eyes because she whispered, "I'm doing an undercover report on detention for the next student council meeting."

Pamela Austin and I have been in chorus together since

the seventh grade. We get along, but the last thing I wanted to do was get into what would likely be a lengthy whispered conversation about who was gonna get the alto solo in the Fall Madrigal concert. I needed to focus all my energy on snagging my new boyfriend. I quickly broke eye contact and started walking toward Chuck when she stage-whispered, "Justin! Sit here!" madly patting the computer chair next to her. I didn't turn back and simply responded with a noncommittal "Hey, Pamela" as I kept moving to the back of the room where Chuck and Becky were. The whole time I was walking down the length of the row, I heard Pamela behind me still patting the seat. Finally I sat down and heard two more soft pats and then silence.

Chuck was at the computer directly in front of me, and Becky was next to him.

I looked at her objectively. Wow. She was so crazily pretty. Long neck, lips she only used ChapStick on because they were naturally the color of an expensive lipstick, reddish gold hair that literally glowed, and a nose all the girls wanted to copy when they got their nose jobs. Her most striking feature was her catlike eyes. Almond shaped and a shade of green that was always changing depending on the light. Add to that a perfectly toned body from years of gymnastics.

Chuck and Becky were the golden couple of our high school. Until they broke up, that is. The student body still hasn't fully recovered from it. Chuck transferred here from Colorado last year, and as soon as they met, they became a steady couple. No matter what time of day, you could always see them making out in all areas of the school: hallway, lunchroom, classroom, football field . . . and once, awkwardly, the boys' locker room (Chuck had smuggled her in there on a dare). I say "awkwardly" because it was the one day I decided to take a shower after gym and I walked, dripping wet, out of the shower and into the locker area wrapped in one of the skimpy school-supplied towels, only to find myself suddenly next to the making-out couple as they were being videotaped for posterity by Doug Gool. That's right, videotaped. As of today, there've been over a thousand YouTube views of them deeply kissing next to a row of gym lockers and then me stumbling up to them with a wet Afro and severe love handles.

Anyway, their breakup last June sent shock waves throughout the entire freshman class, and it wasn't hard to figure out that Becky's dad caused it all. From my signature eavesdropping on various conversations around school and the mall, I found out that he didn't like Chuck from the start. Becky had told him it wasn't a serious relationship, but once he saw the make-out video on YouTube (Becky never cared that it was up because she thought her father was Internet handicapped), he made Becky end their affair *stat*. He picked her up from school that day as usual but didn't wait to get home to start his tirade. No eavesdropping was required on my part because everyone in the building was able to hear him yell from the parking lot, "No daughter of mine is going to ruin her future by having a baby in high school!"

Baby? I thought. *It's not like they were caught having sex.* But apparently seeing his daughter kissing a boy caused visions of teen pregnancy to dance in his head. He made her break up with Chuck that night, and by first period the next day, everyone knew. Chuck and Becky were the power couple of the school and then suddenly it was over. Even the teachers seemed to go through a period of mourning. I don't think her dad actually feared them going all the way, but the real reason he insisted they break up was because Becky was super-smart and her parents have been grooming her for Columbia Medical School (their alma mater) since she was in kindergarten. Instead of going to Jewish summer day camp like I did in elementary school, Becky was enrolled in biology camp. Apparently, they have lab in the morning, flash cards at noon, and then one period in the afternoon for swimming or dissection. Dating a jock was not what her dad envisioned for her. He's an internist and his wife's a pediatrician, and they want to make sure that Becky grows up just like them—that is, marry someone she meets in medical school. I heard Becky talking all about it at lunch one day. No, we were not hanging out; she was with her clutch of beautiful, popular girls and I was one table away, by myself, eating a fluffernutter. (Stop judging my unhealthiness. It was on wheat bread. Well, one piece of wheat and one piece of Wonder.) She said her dad hauled out the saying "A jock retires at age thirty, but a doctor earns forever." I guess that's true, but is money the most important thing in a relationship? Because from what I've seen, a jock's *body* doesn't retire at age thirty. They stay fit for life, as opposed to most doctors. Quite frankly, have you ever checked out the bod on your family doctor? Let's just say most examining rooms don't have free weights.

Poor Becky. It's pretty obvious she doesn't want to go into medicine. My dad is a doctor as well (different hospital from Becky's parents), but he's never pushed me to follow in his footsteps. He knows I want to be on Broadway one day. I not only love musical theater, but I also think that a career is only worth it if you have to struggle, like Mariah Carey did in *Glitter* or Christina Aguilera in *Burlesque*. I always get As in biology without even trying, and medical school seems like it wouldn't be a challenge to me . . . except the staying awake part during boring-ass lectures. I am actually looking forward to the initial rejection after rejection, the struggle to fight my way out of the chorus and become a lead, and finally the reluctant acceptance of all the people who tried to hold me down as they watch me win a Tony Award.

Regardless, Becky's father did not approve of his daughter making out with some studly quarterback who maintained a B-plus average and who was probably going to go to college on a sports scholarship. His daughter was marrying a doctor and that was that.

I sat at the desk and noticed that Chuck and Becky had no schoolbooks open. Students were supposed to do their homework in detention and weren't allowed to use the Internet to check personal email, but we all knew that E.R. and her crippling sciatica wouldn't be able to get up to see what we were actually doing. As I sat down, I noticed that Chuck was logged on to his email. *Hmm,* I thought. *Maybe an old-school instant message is the way to connect with him.*

I typed in my screen name "Broadway4ever" and my password "IheartBroadway" but, like an idiot, forgot to lower the volume of the computer so a booming "You've got mail" filled the room.

I looked up guiltily, waiting to hear the sound of E.R.'s shrill reprimand. I was confused when I saw her simply glaring and waving me up to her desk. Oh yes, I remembered as I walked toward her. *Total vocal rest.* As soon as I stood up, she began writing an obviously hostile note to me. I got to the edge of her desk and started reading the note upside down.

Justin! I'm writing this because my voice is GONE. Yet, each word I write puts an unbelievable strain on my wrist, which is directly connected to my arm, shoulder, neck, and trunk, which therefore makes my sciatica flare up and cause SEVERE lower back pain. But, at the risk of having to get a morphine drip, which my insurance doesn't cover, I will reiterate the detention rules you already know:

NO PERSONAL EMAILS ARE ALLOWED DURING DETEN

Suddenly, another coughing fit started. Hmm . . . somehow writing hurt her throat? Also, if every word put further strain on her sciatica condition, why did she write me a novel? I took the note from the desk during her coughing spasm and finished the word *detention* for her. She shook her head and pointed at me to keep writing. Huh? What was I supposed to add? *Love, Ms. Horvath*? I was momentarily frozen but then took a guess and put an underline beneath NO. She nodded yes but then shook her head no, which I took to mean *You're on the right track but not there yet,* so I added two more lines underneath it. She nodded curtly and I returned to my seat.

As I passed Pamela, I heard her patting the desk next to her again. What was with her? I sat down behind Chuck once more and saw on his computer screen that he and Becky had been writing to each other the whole time I was with Ms. Horvath.

I decided to eavesdrop. Hmm . . . eavesread?

He wrote: What time are you meeting me?

She wrote: Not till after my dad goes to sleep . . . 11?

Meeting? I thought they broke up! Rumor had it that Chuck had met some girl over the summer while he was in Europe with his folks.

Becky's cell phone began to vibrate. She picked it up and whispered "Hello" so Ms. Horvath wouldn't hear. She murmured something, then hung up.

That was Dad. His car is in the shop and he can't pick me up.

Excellent! Let's go out somewhere after detention . . . I want to see you at a normal hour.

Are you crazy? He'll find out. I have to call a cab to take me right home.

C'mon, Becky! Is this gonna go on till we graduate?

It has to. I heard him to say to Mom when they thought I was asleep that if he had to, he'd transfer me to an all-girls school.

Sounds hot.

Ha ha. He means St. Ann's boarding school. You won't be laughing when I'm three towns away!

Don't worry, Beck. If you transferred, I'd go to St. Vincent's.

But what about all our friends? And we won't get any real time alone together. My cousin goes there and said those nuns watch you like hawks.

Wow. My eyes were killing me from reading his screen from my desk. I had to digest it all. So they were still together behind her father's back. It seemed kind of tenuous. If they broke up, then I'd have Chuck to myself. Well, let's just say I'd have more of an *opportunity* to get Chuck to myself. But I couldn't see myself ratting them out to her father just to give me an opening. Even *I* wasn't that devious. Besides, Spencer would have a field day describing the karma I'd get. Maybe I just needed to be patient and let nature take its course. But it was already October, and I vowed this year would be different! This is supposed to be the year of my first kiss. I'm almost sixteen! I've watched the Chuck and Becky video many times, fantasizing that I was the one in his embrace, and it's time for my fantasy to become a reality. I let my mind wander. How cool would it be to date Chuck? If anyone made fun of us, he'd kick their butt. Also, I'd finally be in the popular group, and judging from what I've seen of his make-out technique, my first kiss would be full of fireworks. Of course, I'd feel a little bad for Becky when their thing ends. She's actually a great girl. She's one of the few popular ones who's nice to everyone. Even me. We're both in my favorite class together (theater, natch), and we had a great time last week when we were teamed up together to work on stage kissing. PS, it's easy: If you're the guy, you put your lips to the side of the girl's face and turn her away from the audience so it looks like you're both going at it, but no lips actually touch.

I sat there trying to figure out a way to get to Chuck without being directly responsible for their breakup. Every scenario ended with me getting some divine retribution that caused both mental and physical pain. Why did I ever let Spencer explain karma to me?

Finally, I got it! I'd always been too scared to talk to him, but I realized that I could ease myself into his life without having to actually walk up to him and start an awkward conversation. I knew his screen name from looking over his shoulder.

I quickly typed: Hi, Chuck! It's Justin! What's today's French homework? Forgot! :)

Chuck looked shocked when it appeared on his screen.

He angrily typed: Who are you?

I quickly sent: Look behind you!

He turned.

He turned back.

Who are you?

Oh.

I guess I wasn't quite on his radar.

I reminded him: I'm Justin. I'm in your French class.

He kept staring at the screen.

I added: I was in it last year, too.

No movement.

I sort of got in trouble today for rapping.

He finally started typing: Are you that kid barely wearing the towel in the YouTube video?

That's not the image I wanted in his head, but at least he recognized me.

Yes.

Dude, do some crunches.

Ouch! This wasn't going as planned.

Suddenly, the bell rang. Chuck and Becky signed off and started walking out. Mothereffer! OK, the good news was that I finally conversed with Chuck. Now I had to move to the next level and do it while actually talking. I got my coat on and started running out of the room.

"Justin, wait for me!" It was Pamela, but she was busy wrapping up all of her fifty inches of hair to put underneath her beret.

I've seen this process before and it takes five to ten

minutes. "No time!" I said, turning my head briefly, causing me to bump into Ms. Horvath's desk.

"Ow, my sciatica!" she yelled raspily, which of course led her into a coughing fit. I had no time to wait around and read the angry note she was undoubtedly writing a rough draft of in her head.

Aha! As I raced outside, I saw the loving couple on the front steps of the school. *Uh-oh,* I thought as I skidded to a stop. Once I reached them, what would I do? Even if I asked Chuck for the homework assignment again, I'd get the answer in ten seconds. I needed a reason to hang out with them. I suddenly thought of one as I saw Becky pick up her cell phone and start dialing.

"Hey!" I panted as I walked over and stood next to them. "If either of you needs a lift home, my mom's coming for me."

Becky hung up her cell. "That's sweet of you, Justin." She looked over at Chuck, who shook his head, and then said, "I don't think Chuck does 'cause he lives right behind the school, but I'd love one. If you're sure your mom won't mind."

"Not at all!" I said, proud of my quick thinking.

"Thanks," said Becky.

Silence.

I wanted to talk to Chuck but I couldn't think of anything to say besides "I love you."

"Hey, Becky," I said, to prevent myself from declaring something that was, perhaps, too soon to say, "congrats on that A in Advanced Bio."

She sighed. "I had to study so much for that test my eyes still hurt."

"Really?" I asked. "I didn't think it was that hard."

She rolled her eyes. "Of course you didn't. You always get As in bio, even on surprise quizzes." She laughed without humor. "Maybe my father could adopt you so *you* can be the doctor in the family." She looked over at Chuck and brightened. "Hey, Justin," she said with a wink. "Wanna practice for Mrs. Hall's class?" Mrs. Hall was our theater teacher. I knew immediately what she meant.

"Sure!" I said.

I aggressively grabbed her and dipped her for the fake make-out.

"What the hell!" Chuck yelled.

I suddenly felt on my body two hands I had been fantasizing about touching me. Unfortunately, instead of caressing me, they were forcefully pulling me away from Becky.

"Relax, Chuck!" Becky said, laughing as I caught my breath. "We're practicing stage kissing . . . for acting class. It's not real."

Chuck looked embarrassed . . . and gorgeous.

"Anyway," she said, obviously for my benefit, "why should you care? We're broken up."

I already knew the real deal but didn't comment.

Chuck nodded and said stiffly, "You're right, Becky. We are."

Ouch. If that was his version of convincing, maybe *he* was the one who needed acting class.

"OK, Becks," he said awkwardly. "So, uh . . . I guess I'll see you when that report is due. Around eleven."

That didn't make any sense, but I knew what his clunky cover-up really meant. I was annoyed that he was about to leave. My plan was not to wait here with Becky but to get some quality time with Chuck. I heard a car turning into the school lot. I looked and saw that it wasn't my mom's. It was some kind of red sports car.

"Oh no!" said Becky in a frightened whisper. "It's my father!"

"I thought his car was broken," I said.

"He's driving my mother's car. She must have come home early."

She suddenly looked at me and we both realized that she never told me about her father's car being in the shop. I had read it on Chuck's computer screen.

She looked at me quizzically. "How did you know—"

"Becky!" Her dad walked up with a big smile. He was an imposing six foot three with a youthful, handsome face but completely silver hair. "I'm so glad I caught you. You called a cab—"

He cut off abruptly when he saw Chuck. He turned toward Becky. His whole face changed. What had been open and friendly was now closed and steaming mad.

"What is he doing here?" he demanded.

"He's a student in this school, Dad!" Becky said, exasperated.

"Don't take that tone with me, young lady. You know that your mother and I forbade you from seeing him anymore."

Chuck stepped up to her father. "Dr. Phillips, we broke up last June like you wanted. We just happened to have detention today."

Her father's eyes narrowed. "You also just happened to be at Ben and Jerry's that night I saw both of you. And at the Gap. And at the footbridge by the lake."

Becky looked nervous. "Dad, stop! Chuck lives in this town. I can't help it if he sometimes goes for ice cream or to the mall."

Her father was silent. Then it looked like he made a decision.

"No, Becky, you can't control the fact that he's always nearby. However, *I* can." He pointed his finger at her. "I'm taking you out of this school and enrolling you somewhere you can focus on your academics and *not* on the local quarterback."

Becky looked stricken. So did I. If she transferred, it meant that Chuck would transfer, too. I couldn't lose my boyfriend before I stole him.

"Dr. Phillips," I said desperately, "you have to believe that Becky isn't dating Chuck anymore."

He looked at me quizzically. "Aren't you Dr. Goldblatt's son?"

I smiled. "Yes, sir. I am."

He looked pleased. "I see your father at conferences often. Apparently"—he winked at me—"you're a bio whiz."

Oy. I hated it when my father bragged about my bio grades. Especially since I didn't care about that crap at all. I wanted the Great White Way, not the alimentary canal.

He looked me up and down. "You're a nice kid. Academically sound, obviously a gentleman . . . unlike some students." He glared at Chuck and then looked back at me. "But why should I believe you?"

I looked at Chuck. He looked blank.

I looked at Becky. She looked devastated.

I realized what I had to do.

I stood next to Becky. "I know for a fact that Becky is through dating Chuck because"—I gave Becky an intense look, hoping she knew where I was going with this—"your daughter is now dating me!"

I turned toward her and immediately pulled her into our stage kiss. We held it for ten seconds and disengaged. Becky grabbed my hand and turned toward her father.

He was smiling.

RIGHT AFTER I "KISSED" BECKY, I said a quick goodbye to her and excused myself to her dad by saying that I had a big bio exam to study for. I called my mom and told her I didn't need a lift, and sprinted home. I had to make an emergency escape before her dad could question me. What if he asked me if I was serious about Becky? Or if we were going to the Spring Fling together? I didn't want to give the wrong answer, so I skedaddled. I assumed her dad would very quickly see through our charade, but hopefully I had impressed Chuck with my quick thinking so that he'd feel he owed me something . . . something like a night on the town or a severe make-out session.

I stayed in my room for hours waiting for the phone to ring, my thoughts alternating between fear of Dr. Phillips yelling at me for lying and hope that Chuck would want to thank me. Finally I decided to go to bed and fell asleep replaying everything that had happened in front of the school, sometimes substituting Chuck's face for Becky's in the final embrace. And by "sometimes" I mean "every time."

Walking to school the next morning, I saw Becky waiting in front of the Roasted Bean.

"Here," she said with a big grin while holding out a large to-go cup.

I took a sip and smiled. "How'd you know I love vanilla lattes?"

"How would I *not* know what my boyfriend drinks?" she asked.

Ha ha. I thought it was sweet that she wanted to thank me for yesterday.

I took another sip. Wow! She even put in six packets of Sugar in the Raw, just the way I like it. "OK, spill. How long did it take your father to figure it out?"

She laughed-snorted. "Are you kidding me? He's so desperate for me to be with a future doctor, he'd believe I was dating Dr. Phil."

She clutched my hand.

Wait a minute. Did *she* think we were dating?

She looked apologetic. "I know you usually like a double shot in the latte, but I ran out of money."

What was happening? How did she know so much about me? Was I starring in an M. Night Shyamalan flick? And is that how you spell his last name? And does the *M.* stand for "Mid"?

She laughed. "Don't look so scared. Chuck and I went to your Facebook page last night, and he quizzed me until I memorized everything." She started counting off things on her fingers. "Favorite drink: vanilla latte. Favorite all-time comedienne: Lucille Ball. Favorite all-time Broadway star: Patti LuPone."

Not quite . . .

". . . tied with Betty Buckley."

Wow! She was good. "I'm impressed!" I said. "And confused."

She grabbed my hand again. "Listen, Justin," she said as we started walking, "I know it's a big imposition, but if you and I could pretend that we're dating, even for just a little while, it would really help me out." Her pleading face looked so beautiful in the early-morning sunlight, I could see why Chuck loved her. "If my dad thinks we're dating, he won't keep checking up on me."

The latte started to make sense. "I get it now. You were memorizing my Facebook profile so if your dad asks you questions about me, you'll know how to answer."

Her eyes lit up—that is, they went from shining to sparkling. "Exactly!"

We passed by the park where Spencer and I first revealed to each other that we were gay. There was a group of young moms wheeling their babies in expensive carriages while wearing designer sweatpants and ankle weights.

I thought about it. I liked her. She'd always been nice to me. But I didn't feel like spending a month, or however long she wanted, tricking her dad. It would definitely require some work on my part and take me away from my real goals—leaving my loser status and snagging Chuck. How would being her pretend boyfriend help me become his real one?

She kept talking. "Every time I leave the house, I'm scrutinized. But if my dad thinks I'm meeting you, he won't care. I can go out every night."

"And you'll meet Chuck instead," I said enviously.

"Well, I'll meet both of you."

WHAT?

"Both of us?" I managed to get out.

"Well, I can say I'm meeting you for dinner with some friends. Those 'friends' will be Chuck."

I'd be hanging out with Chuck every night? "Um . . . ," I said slowly. I didn't want to sound too desperate. Plus it's hard to talk with drool in your mouth.

I swallowed. "What if your dad finds out Chuck is with us?"

She shook her head. "I actually don't think he'd care. He is so certain you're perfect for me, an actual bio whiz, he couldn't imagine I'd still be interested in Chuck." She looked me up and down. "You represent total trustworthiness to him. I don't think he sees you as a threat to my virginity."

That was truer than he even thought.

"As long as people think we're dating, he'll let me off his tight leash."

"What do you mean 'people'? Who besides your parents?"

"Justin! The only way to make this valid is for everyone to believe it . . . not just my dad."

All the kids in school were supposed to believe I'm dating Becky? I'm known as the school poster boy for gayness. And out-of-shapeness. No one would believe that Becky was into me.

She snapped in front of my face to bring me out of my trance. "I know what you're thinking, and we just have to do that Nazi shtick."

What? I'm Jewish! I'm certainly willing to pretend I'm straight to gain popularity, but a member of the Third Reich? Am I that desperate?

"What kind of a Nazi shtick?" I asked. "The fun Mel Brooks kind? Or the unfun Joseph Goebbels kind?"

Becky laughed. And an angel got her wings. "I don't *literally* mean be a Nazi, silly!" She said it kind of loudly, prompting a glare from a passing elderly couple. "I mean we have to adopt that technique we just learned about in social studies."

Oh! She meant the Nazi Big Lie technique. The Nazis would make up a lie and repeat it over and over fervently, without wavering, until people started believing it. We also learned that it was a technique used by our own Bush administration. Hmm . . . I guess that was one way they kicked it old-school. I tried it only once on my mom ("I was *not* on YouTube watching old Tony Award clips until three a.m. on a school night!") but discovered that it doesn't work when your mom literally walks in on you watching said Tony Award clips at three a.m. on a school night. That was my only foray into using that technique and it had failed miserably. Dare I try it again? Would any kid in this school buy me as being straight? Or believe that Becky would choose me after the hotness that is Chuck?

As if Becky read my mind, she said, "Let's see if it works. Here comes Savannah Lichtenstein."

Savannah is wealthy and gorgeous, with perfectly high-lighted blond hair, but despite her money and looks, she's stuck in a high-middle social echelon because her mom fancies herself an undiscovered designer and makes all of Savannah's school outfits. Her clothes are actually always great-looking but obviously never have any of the designer labels that the girls at our school covet. In fact, the only label her clothes sport is a big *Lichtenstein* that her mother sews onto every outfit, always in a different spot. It doesn't quite carry the same clout as, say, Versace. But it does have almost double the letters for maximum awkwardness. This time I spotted the *Lichtenstein* on the bottom left cuff of her flared pants. She was coming down the block perpendicular to us and we were all approaching the same corner.

"Hey, Savannah!" Becky said as she waved.

"Hey, Becky . . ."

As Savannah walked up to us, I could tell she trying to decide whether to just say hello to Becky or if she also had to say hello to me. If I had just happened to walk by at that moment, she would have ignored me, but since I really was walking with Becky, she knew she had to acknowledge me. She looked back and forth between Becky and me and suddenly—

"Hi, Justin," she finally said.

Wow. Already my social standing went up a notch. I don't think Savannah's spoken to me since the sixth-grade production of *Grease*. And that was only onstage because she was Frenchie to my Doody. Before "Hi, Justin," the last words she spoke directly to me were "Sandy and Danny belong together!"

Becky admired her outfit. "I love the flare in the pants, don't you?"

"My mom—" Savannah started to answer, but then realized that Becky was asking me.

I let the moment of shock register on her face and then turned toward Becky and answered, "Yeah . . . very eighties."

Becky playfully hit my arm. "Seventies, you ninny!" She turned to Savannah and pointed at me playfully. "This one doesn't know anything about fashion." She grabbed my hand. "Thank God he's so cute."

Savannah's face was frozen, mouth agape and upper eyelids as far away from the lower lids as possible. Becky ignored the fact that Savannah's eyes were now as flared as her pants and asked her, "You wanna walk to school with us?"

"With . . . both of you?" she asked. She looked at our intertwined hands. "I didn't know you guys were . . ." She faded out. She started again. "Are you guys . . . ?" Needing clarification, she spoke slowly. "Shouldn't we wait for Chuck?"

"For what?" asked Becky, with a combination of innocence, sweetness, and a sprinkling of pixie dust.

Savannah was now acting as if a gasket had blown inside her logic area. She kept opening and closing her mouth and finally sputtered, "Aren't you . . . ? Isn't Chuck your . . . ?"

"My boyfriend?" Becky finished the sentence for her. "Not for a loooong time. Where have you been?" She laughed with a slightly mocking edge to make Savannah feel out of the loop.

"But you faked—" Savannah lowered her voice. "I know you pretended to break up last year to get your father off your case. . . ."

Becky nodded.

"But," Savannah continued, "I thought you were still dating."

Becky looked at me and rolled her eyes. "Savannah, Chuck and I broke up for real back in . . ." She let her sentence die off and then laughed. "I've been dating Justin for a while now. I can't believe you didn't know." She gave Savannah a slightly pitying shake of her head.

"I had no i— I mean, no one told me. . . ." Savannah didn't know how to play it. Up until one minute ago, she had thought Chuck and Becky were still secretly dating. But now, if she acknowledged that she had no idea about Becky dating me, it would imply that she wasn't hanging out with the "cool" kids who supposedly *did* know. I could see her make a decision in her mind.

Savannah motioned toward both of us. "I mean, I *knew* about you and Justin. . . ."

She did?

"I just didn't know how serious it was." She smiled warmly.

Becky kissed my cheek. "It's very serious."

Savannah grinned. "Duh!"

Wow. I was in awe of Becky's technique. She just made a person claim they had always known something that had, in fact, never been true. I guess having a crazy father whom you're constantly trying to trick has some benefits.

We started walking toward school, and I could tell Savannah was super-happy to be included in Becky's presence. I felt the same way. It was a little like walking with the queen. Everyone smiled and waved as we passed . . . which was then followed by a double take when they saw Becky holding hands with me.

"What's your social studies report gonna be about?" Savannah asked. "I'm doing the Civil War."

I waited for Becky to answer. Then I realized they were both staring at me. Savannah was talking to *me*—uninitiated!

Immobilization overtook me. I wasn't really sure how to chat with someone who was in a higher social stratum than myself. I'm used to having conversations with those in my own lowly status and being ignored by everyone else. I decided to answer like I normally would.

"I'm doing a report on McCarthyism in the fifties."

"Oh . . . ," she said, trailing off.

Silence. UGH! I was so annoyed with myself! I finally had a chance to converse with someone who wasn't considered a total loser by the whole school and I was blowing it. I felt like I was solidifying my lowly social standing. How could I make her think I had risen in the ranks? In my head, I ran through conversations I had eavesdropped on in the past. Hmm . . . it seemed the people at the top always had a certain style when they spoke to anyone lower than them. I decided to give it a try. "You're doing the Civil War?" I asked while adopting a slight sneer. "Why'd you pick something stupid like that?"

Was I doing it right?

"I know," she said, shaking her head. "I'm an idiot sometimes."

That was it! I had to be a little mean to show I was above her. Then she'd wanna keep talking.

She rolled her eyes. "I don't know what I was thinking. Maybe I can still switch. What do you think I should write about?"

Uh-oh. In reality, I thought the Civil War was fascinating, so I didn't have an immediate follow-up. "Um . . ." I blurted out the first thing that came to my mind. "The Nazi Big Lie technique."

Becky quickly joined in the conversation. "Oh, just ignore him, Savannah. He thinks everything's boring if it doesn't involve biology."

"Or Broadway," I added.

"Or girls!" Becky added, probably to counteract my last

comment. I didn't know how *that* Nazi big lie was gonna fly until Savannah laughed and said, "Typical guy."

Typical guy?! I'd always been the outcast, the loser, the weirdo. *Never* "typical." My life seemed to be on a completely new path, and I was going to stay on it! God bless Mr. Plotnick's social studies class. Because if we hadn't spent that week on World War II, Becky and I wouldn't have learned the theory that if you state something with full confidence, even a blatant lie, *people will believe you.*

Wow. I never imagined I would one day say this, but . . . thank you, Nazis!

5

COINCIDENTALLY, MY FIRST CLASS WAS social studies and nothing seemed different—aka I was ignored by the cool/popular/smart kids and harassed by the Doug Gool group. Today, class started with a lesson about World War II's Axis of Evil, and not surprisingly, Doug taped a note to the back of my seat that said "Axis of Gayvil." World War II has been especially ripe for Doug to find harassment material. Besides learning the Nazi Big Lie technique over the last few weeks, we also learned about the airplane that dropped the atomic bomb: the devastatingly named (for me) *Enola Gay*. As soon as class was out that day, Doug and his friends started calling me "Enola." I, of course, made the mistake of asking them not to call me that, so they offered to be more polite and started calling me Miss Gay. I knew if I protested "Miss Gay," it would then become "*Ms.* Gay," so I quit before I was addressed as a feminist.

At the beginning of class, I saw Doug put a piece of

chocolate on Mary Ann Cortale's (the guidance counselor's daughter) seat, and she sat down without seeing it. We spent the second half of class learning about Hitler's girlfriend (Eva Braun). When the bell rang, Mary Ann got up with the chocolate flattened all across the left butt cheek of one of her two signature outfits. On the way out, I braced myself for a Doug Gool onslaught but thankfully he forgot about the Axis of Gayvil and instead stood behind Mary Ann and said, "Look, everyone. It's Eva *Brown*!" Doug's two cronies high-fived him and some kids not in Doug's group started to laugh, too. Mary Ann looked around, confused. She knew they were making fun of her but didn't know why, because she couldn't see the chocolate. I didn't want to attract any Doug attention, plus I was dying to know if word of my "relationship" with Becky had spread, so I started to sneak out.

When I was by the door, I saw Spencer push through the circle of kids that was starting to surround Mary Ann. He stood in front of her, handed her a tissue, and said simply, "You have chocolate on the back of your dress." As Mary Ann turned around to wipe it, she tripped a little and her glasses fell to the ground and cracked. People stopped laughing as she bent down to pick them up. She managed to wipe the chocolate with one hand while grabbing her glasses with the other, but as she got up, her organic rubber band snagged on the desk, which made her hair disengage from its signature ponytail. She stood there with her hair askew, holding her ruined glasses in one hand and a dirty tissue in the other. The crowd that was around her began to disperse. They didn't mind mocking and psychologically torturing her, but actual physical damage wasn't in the mix when you were considered a "good kid" by your parents.

The only ones who remained were Spencer and Doug Gool. I looked at them and then looked back at Mary Ann. I didn't mean to be shallow at that moment, but seeing her without her thick glasses and with her hair less severe made me realize that she actually had a beautiful face. It was like that cliché I've seen in old black-and-white movies with the librarian letting down her hair to reveal herself as a knockout, but it was true. Spencer was helping Mary Ann get herself together and Doug was watching. For a second, I thought there was going to be a Hallmark moment where Doug sees the broken glasses and realizes the damage his words can do. He then puts out his hand to Mary Ann and says, "Friends?"

And . . . credits.

That didn't happen. Instead of putting out his hand, he simply put out a finger. I think you know the one. After that, he got his book bag, bumped Spencer in the shoulder (calling him a spaz), and walked out. I watched Doug go down the hallway and was pleasantly surprised to see Chuck coming from the other direction. I gazed at him as he stopped in front of me and said to one of his friends in the classroom, "See you at lunch, right?"

Sigh. He's so handsome. He was sporting just a little bit of facial hair, and I noticed that, like his hair, his beard was sandy blond but with a hint of red in it as well. I got a great view because he kept standing in front of me. I didn't know why his friend hadn't responded until I realized the only people left in the classroom were Spencer and Mary Ann.

AH! *I* was the friend he wanted to see at lunch! I quickly changed my facial expression from *staring from afar* to *responding from close up* and answered, "Yes, Chuck. I will see you at lunch." It was a little stilted but, come on, I was in shock! This was the first time he had ever asked me a question that wasn't laced with annoyance or anger. Spencer and I always ate lunch together, so did this mean that Chuck would "see" me as he walked to his table, or did he mean that both he and Becky would actually be sitting with us? Dare I hope for such joy?

Before I could ask, Chuck gave me a thumbs-up (such cute thumbs!) and walked off while I went toward my locker in a daze. When I got there, I realized I hadn't said goodbye to Spencer, but I knew I'd see him at lunch and would explain everything. The bell rang and I ran to study hall next and then to computer lab, where nobody spoke to anybody because we were all wearing headphones, trying to upload sound effects into the games we were creating. PS, my computer game was Broadway themed (natch) and took place on the streets of New York. As the player, you were an up-and-coming actor and had to sabotage older established stars. The more stars you got rid of, the more room there was for you to become famous. You had the option of pushing them down stairs, pushing them in front of taxis, or pushing them into the lake at Central Park.

(I tried for the ol' making-scenery-collapse-on-them trick or electrocuting them with their own microphone but could only figure out how to program a push move on the computer.)

I spent the whole period trying to get the perfect sound for being pushed in front of a cab. I wanted a scream, a tire screech, and the cabdriver yelling, "Son of a—"

Unfortunately, I only had the option of using a computerized voice, which made it sound like the cab was being driven by a robot. Or by Madonna acting in a film. (If you don't know what I mean, rent *Shanghai Surprise*.)

Finally, the bell rang and I skedaddled to lunch.

Mmm. Delicious pizza. The lunch lady likes me (and knows I'm a vegetarian), so she orders soy pepperoni just for me and puts a ton of pieces on my slice. I thanked her, picked up a cookie for dessert (and by "a" cookie I mean "three"), and saw Spencer sitting at our usual table. I was on my way over to give him the lowdown when I heard my name yelled. I looked around and realized it was coming from Cool U.

Oh no.

Cool U is the name Spencer and I call the table where all the popular kids sit. It's right next to the window that looks out onto the football field. Not to be confused with Toughs 'R' Us, which is the table by the cereal bar where Doug Gool and his friends sit. I braced myself for the mean comment that usually follows contact from anyone at either table. Hmm. Nothing. I waited and then heard my name yelled again. I quickly glanced over and saw a fist waving in the air.

AH!!!

Wait a minute . . . It wasn't a fist. It was a hand. Belonging to Savannah. It was waving me over. Was it a trap? I slowly walked toward the table and stopped.

Savannah stood up.

"Come on, Justin! I saved you a seat." She pointed to a seat on the boys' side, right next to the window. Cool U is a segregated table. On one side sit all of the cheerleaders/popular girls and on the other side, all the jocks/cool boys. Opposite "my" seat was an empty chair that I assumed Savannah was saving for Becky. I didn't know what to do. I took a few steps closer.

"Hi, Justin."

"Hey, Justin."

"What up, J?"

What the—? Everyone on the girls' side looked up from their food (aka lettuce leaves with no-cal dressing) and gave me a little wave and greeting as I got nearer. The sound was new to my ears because I had never heard my name said by their voices. Wow. *That's* what it sounds like when a popular girl says "Justin." All the girls who had ignored me for the last ten years were now greeting me like we were old friends. I guess Savannah the Gossip Machine had gotten the word out. Hearing all this newfound friendliness gave me the strength to walk to the edge of the table. I looked back at Spencer's table and saw that he was sitting with Mary Ann. That did it. I didn't want to spend my whole lunch comforting her.

I took a big step closer and then kept walking. Wow. I had

never entered the realm of that table. I had only seen it from afar. Weird. It had always seemed higher and longer than the ones I sat at, but as I got closer, I realized it was the same type of table as the others in the cafeteria. I decided to stop feeling nervous. After all, the girls were so inviting. I then looked at the opposite side of the table. Uh-oh. Unfortunately, Savannah's big mouth had only funneled toward the girls. The boys were all looking at me with confusion and mounting anger. When I finally got to the empty seat, I stood behind it. Dare I sit down? The guys started snickering and looking at each other. I could tell they were trying to decide who was going to tell me to get the hell away and how violent it was gonna be. Suddenly, I hear, "Yo, Justin! Just in time!" Huh? When did Savannah's voice get so manly, and quite frankly, sexy?

Whoa!

It wasn't Savannah. It was Chuck, who magically appeared and was standing behind the seat next to my empty one. Now the guys' faces were even more confused. If the dictionary needed a visual to go with the definition of "WTF???" they could all be models.

"Come on, guys. Make some room." Chuck pushed the boy next to him, and all the guys moved their chairs a little. Chuck put down his tray, pulled out his chair, and sat down. He patted the seat next to him and I gingerly sat in it.

There was silence.

"Yo, guys." Chuck turned toward the boys' side. "Don't feel weird. I'm cool with it."

Silence.

That comment apparently sent them all into a state of shock. The boys expected him to say something along the lines of "Let's get 'im" or at least, "Leave him alone." But hearing him say "I ain't jealous" was so unexpected, I don't think anyone actually understood what he said. It's as if he'd turned to them and suddenly spoke a different language. The boys all looked at each other. Chuck then turned back toward me and started talking. But not really. His mouth was moving, but I couldn't understand what he was saying.

"What???" I finally said.

"Exactly," he replied, and then kept up his mumbling.

What was happening? I looked around and saw that all the boys were leaning over the table toward someone on the girls' side. The person they were leaning toward was Savannah. Aha! I got it. Chuck wanted to give the boys some time to hear the news. I looked up again and saw that Savannah was now talking to Ted, the star pitcher on the baseball team. She laughed snottily and asked, "Didn't you know?"

Everyone looked at him. Uh-oh. What if he said what was obvious? No, he hadn't heard it because *it's not true*! I started to sweat. Was I about to be evicted from Cool U? I quickly glanced at Spencer's table. Was I going to have to spend the rest of this lunch with Mary Ann Cortale comforting *me*?

Ted looked at Chuck.

Ted looked at me.

Finally he shrugged and said to Savannah, "Of course I knew. But I didn't know it was so serious."

WHAT?

That's *exactly* what Savannah said when Becky tried the same technique. Wow. No wonder Germany almost took over the world. Suddenly, I smelled roses, ylang-ylang, and fresh laundry. Sure enough, Becky arrived carrying her lunch: a slice of pizza and French fries. She was frustratingly one of those people who could eat anything and still have an amazing figure. She sat down in the seat that Savannah had saved for her and then leaned across the table. I didn't know why she was infiltrating the boys' side until she said, "Hi, honey," and came in for a kiss. I leaned to the right so she could kiss Chuck but then realized that *I* was supposed to be "honey." Help! I didn't have time to lean all the way back to the left, so she wound up kissing the air between Chuck and me.

She turned to Savannah. "That's my Justin. He hates PDA." I knew she meant "public displays of affection" and not "personal digital assistants," but, ironically, I do hate being with someone who's making out right next to me *or* constantly typing on their phone. So the acronym was correct on two levels.

"That's why he never sits here," she went on. She looked at me and winked. "Don't worry, Justin. I remember my vow!" I nodded like I knew what she meant. She turned back to the other girls. "I promised him there'd be no mushy stuff if he'd sit here just this once."

What a trickster! She was acting like it's been my choice

that I haven't sat at Cool U instead of the fact that I've never dared leave the loser table for fear of being forced to eat my teeth for lunch. I could tell everyone was processing all of this new information.

Oscar Kota, known throughout the school for tackling and "accidentally" knocking out Syosset High School's quarterback, looked at Becky and then back at me. He suddenly shook his head like he was trying to get rid of a crazy thought that had wormed its way in there. I could tell he needed clarification.

He pointed his finger at both of us. "You're telling us that you . . . are dating?"

Suddenly everyone started looking at us.

Uh-oh. Were they on to us? I thought the Nazi Big Lie technique had a shelf life longer than two minutes!

"Of course we're dating!" Becky said with a smile. But it wasn't really a smile. She just moved her lips so her teeth showed.

"Yeah," I said, avoiding eye contact and adding more liquid to my already sweaty shirt. "Of course we are."

No one said anything. I could see Becky was avoiding the situation by staring at her pizza, and I was almost ready to make a mad dash to Spencer's table when suddenly Chuck piped up.

"Of course they're dating, bozo!" He lightly punched the guy on the shoulder.

That did it. There was more silence, then a moment where I could tell everyone collectively decided to drop it. The guys went back to their pizza and the girls started moving greens around their plates and chattering. Phew. It looked like they were buying it for the time being, but that last minute had been scary! If our ruse fell apart before it really began, I could forget about having private time with Chuck that would lead to him eventually experimenting with a boy-on-boy kiss. I knew that for this fakery to really work, we'd need a strong base of believability. Becky and I obviously crack under pressure, and we can't always rely on Chuck to save us. Hmm. I needed to think of a reason *why* Becky would be with me. That way people wouldn't have to keep believing something that literally made no sense.

I sat and thought: Why would she date me after being with Chuck? It certainly wasn't because of my bod, my hair, or my braces-covered teeth. Was there *any* part of me I found physically attractive?

No.

Not that I'm ugly. I know that when I get older, my looks will come together. But right now, I'm in the period affectionately known as the "awkward years" but that should be known as the "fugly years."

Why date anyone if not for their looks?

Wait.

I remembered watching the Tony Awards last year and there was a shot of a nominated actor in the audience who was bald and whose body made me look like Adonis. I had read online that he was gay and thought to myself, *Yowtch. Even though I'd love to date a Broadway star one day, I could never bring myself to kiss that guy.*

Later on, there was a live performance from his show and it turned out he was an AMAZING performer. *So* funny, SUCH a great voice, and, even though he was heavy, he was a sassy dancer. Suddenly, all I wanted to do was date him! I mentioned it to Spencer the next day, and he told me I had what's called a talent crush. That's when you're not attracted to a person when you first see them, but their talent is such a turn-on that you want to go out with them.

Hmm. *I* had talent! Should I get onto the table and launch into my swing choir solo? There was a dance that went with it as well. Maybe everyone would think Becky was into me because of my amazing high notes and Broadway moves.

And cut.

Even *I* knew that was pushing it. It would be one thing if all the cool kids came to a chorus concert and were impressed when they saw me in action, but I knew *that* would only happen on opposite day, which seems to only exist on those horrible sitcoms aimed at tweens.

That got me thinking of one time during a sleepover with Spencer when I went into a whole tirade because his younger sister was watching one of those shows. Overhearing those clanky lines followed by loud, prerecorded guffaws made me so angry! After fifteen minutes, I'd had it. I found my iPod, waited for an unfunny line (I didn't have to wait long), and recorded the long fake laugh that followed it.

Later that night, I demonstrated what those awful sitcoms did by reciting the most boring thing I knew to Spencer and then adding the laugh track I had recorded. I read our geometry theorems list in the voices of the two leading girl actresses, followed by the laugh track.

The bubbly blonde: *Natasha! The area of a triangle is half that of a parallelogram standing on the same base and between the same parallels.* (LAUGH TRACK)

The boy-crazy brunette: *But, Amber! Through any point outside a line, one and only one perpendicular can be drawn to the given line.* (LAUGH TRACK)

Spencer started laughing, so just to push it, I found the list of venereal disease symptoms we had to memorize for health class and kept the scene going.

Amber: *Natasha! Loss of hair and small pustules with milky discharge!* (LAUGH TRACK)
Natasha: *But, Amber! Dry mouth and burning or itching in the urethra.* (LAUGH TRACK)

We literally laughed about that the whole night.
YES!
That's it! I could make someone laugh for a whole night. That was a talent, too. Everyone will think Becky has a talent crush on me because I'm funny. Case closed.

Wait. I just realized. The kids at Cool U have never actually heard me be funny. My contact with them has mostly consisted of me:

a. not speaking in class.
b. not speaking when I pass them in the hallway.
c. not speaking when I see them at the mall.
All under the umbrella of:
d. never being spoken to by them.

OK. I had to do something funny. But what?

My thought-fest was broken by Oscar yelling in Chuck's direction, "Yo, bro. Don't forget practice starts fifteen minutes earlier today."

Chuck was chewing so he couldn't respond right away.

An inspiration hit me and I suddenly spoke, doing my best Chuck imitation: "Yeah, well, I can't play today. I left my jockstrap in your mother's bed."

Everyone laughed. Even Chuck and Oscar.

"That sounded just like Chuck!" Savannah said, stating the obvious.

It wasn't hard for me. I obsessed so much about that Greek god that I knew how to make my voice sound exactly like his.

"Do someone else!" Becky said.

Uh-oh. I panicked. I didn't have any other imitations in my arsenal. Then I realized that doing a funny imitation wasn't enough for acceptance from this group. I needed one final ingredient: meanness.

"I don't have time to do any more imitations, Becky. I have to throw out that pile of rags." I indicated something unpleasant across the table.

"What pile of rags?" Becky asked, confused.

I squinted, then said, "Oops. I didn't see the *Lichtenstein* stitched on the side. Sorry, Savannah!"

Everyone looked at Savannah's outfit and laughed. Savannah turned red but then joined in.

I did it!

Everyone really believed I was dating Becky. Well, the Nazi Big Lie set it up but I solidified it. I knew enough to "leave 'em laughing," so I got up with my tray to get some (more) dessert. As I was walking away, I saw Chase Sheerin walk up to the table. He's a junior and a major jock who's planning on graduating a year early. He only has half a lunch period because he's doubling up classes. He walked over to my seat and put his tray down. Oh no. My popularity lasted only five minutes.

Suddenly, I saw Oscar say something to Chase. Then all the boys shifted their chairs to the left and Chase got up and got himself another chair.

Oscar saved my seat? And all the guys moved down? And Chuck didn't even have to say anything?

I took a deep breath.

My life had changed.

I belonged at Cool U!

6

I COULD NOW DIVIDE MY life into pre- and post-membership in Cool U. Everything was suddenly different. I had English right after lunch. Usually I sit at my desk before the bell rings, quickly reading Playbill.com on my phone to see the latest Broadway update. Today, however, I hung out with Oscar and Ted (!) and talked about the upcoming game (!!). Unfortunately, I don't know anything about sports, so I wasn't sure if the so-called upcoming game was baseball, football, or from what few terms I half understood, some version of polo played on an ice rink that's melted. Regardless, I nodded a lot and pretended to laugh when they made fun of Chase. When I got nervous they were going to ask me a question I couldn't answer about the sport, I did an imitation of Chuck dancing around and saying, "Look, everyone! I blocked a goal!" I don't know if they laughed because there's no goal in the game they were talking about or because Chuck isn't the blocker, but, regardless, I got a laugh and the bell rang.

Once class began, it was hard for me to concentrate because faking that conversation took so much energy. But I got my energy back walking through the hallway after class—it was exciting having *so* many people say hi to me. I was actually late for my next class because Savannah stopped to tell me some gossip about Julianne Taylor. Turns out, Julianne wasn't really dating that guy she met on a teen tour—she's never even been *on* a teen tour! Savannah wanted to plan how we could trip her up at her own game tomorrow at lunch. I was shocked at first because I thought Savannah and Julianne were great friends, but then I remembered Oscar and Ted making fun of Chase before English class. I guess all the cool kids are friends when they're together, but when someone isn't there they get talked about. I'm as dishy as the next (out-of-shape) fifteen-year-old, but the cool kids seemed to go further than I do.

I wondered why I'd want to eat at Cool U if it meant all those kids were going to say mean things about me when I wasn't around, but I quickly dismissed that thought as Spencer-think and put it out of my head. Spencer believes that even light gossip is "bad for your chi" ever since he started "working on himself" this year. His newest thing is claiming he'd never say anything behind someone's back he wouldn't say to his or her face, but that seems waaaay too general for me. I see the effort it takes for him not to join in when I make fun of how Pamela Austin sounds on her chorus solo. For the winter concert, we're singing a medley of old American folk songs, and for some reason Pamela uses a crazy pseudo-Cockney accent on her solo. She's constantly singing, "Oh, I come from Alabam*er* with a banjo on *me* knee." Our conductor has corrected her so many times, but when Pamela gets into the music, she forgets and lets loose with her crazy accent. I do an amazing imitation of her and I can tell Spencer wants to laugh, but he just shakes his head instead. Lately he reminds me of my grandfather, who always shakes his head and has the same comment about every story in the news: "It's different now. It's all different."

Speaking of Spencer, right after school, I texted him to see if I could come over. He wrote that he had a planning meeting for a rally against Walmart but he'd be home by four-thirty. Ever since I've known him, he's been protesting against big corporations that don't treat their workers fairly. When we were in sixth grade, he missed graduation so he could go to a "day of outrage" against Sam's Club. I've always begged him to focus more on protesting things that I could benefit from. Like husky jeans. Why do I want the label on my jeans to reiterate what people are already seeing? They get it; I'm overweight. Why can't they be renamed "thin jeans" so people can at least question whether they should believe their own eyes?

Regardless, after the final bell rang, I ran home to practice my violin. My mom was, of course, sitting in front of her computer when I came in.

"Hi, honey," she said as she waved me over. "Look!" She pointed proudly to the screen. An enormous A in twenty-four-point font was on top of the "paper" she had emailed in last week for her American history course.

"Congratulations, Mom!" I gave her a peck on the cheek. I stood back so I could drop my bomb. "Actually, I have big news, too."

She looked at me expectantly.

"I'm dating Becky Phillips!" I smiled broadly and waited, knowing she would need time to figure out how to react.

She kept looking at me with the same expression, waiting for the follow-up. I hated that I had to go through this charade with her, but I felt I had to tell her in case she ran into Becky's dad. If he brought it up and my parents didn't know anything, it would make her dad suspicious. But I couldn't tell her about my crush on Chuck because she'd ruin any chance of something really happening. Here's why:

Even though I've never officially told her that I'm gay, I'm pretty sure that both she and my dad know. I've just been too scared to tell them. I don't think they'll judge me for being gay (they're good friends with a lesbian couple they've known since college, and my dad works with plenty of gay doctors), but I've kept my trap shut because it's impossible to predict what situation they'll turn into an opportunity to "help out."

Some parents go on date nights or take samba classes; my mom and dad love to team up and "fix" problems.

Unfortunately, it always ends with them feeling fantastic, contrasted with the mortification of the person they're helping. I've never spoken to my dad's colleagues or friends directly about it, but I've seen it in action. One time, my dad overheard (aka eavesdropped on—where do you think *I* learned it from?) a nurse in the hospital cafeteria complaining to one of the physical therapists that she hadn't had a birthday party since she was a kid. That night, he and my mom decided to plan an elaborate surprise party for her. For weeks, I could hear them giggling in the kitchen as they mapped it all out. My dad was able to get his hands on the nurse's cell phone when she was on her rounds, and he invited friends from her contact list. That specific move wound up completely backfiring, but it led to a great acting lesson for me. When the nurse unwittingly walked into the party, I was able to study what two versions of surprise looked like: The jarringly shocked/vaguely happy surprise she wore on her face when people shouted "Happy Birthday" and the horrified/trapped/furious surprise when she saw her ex-boyfriend in the room.

The party wound up being fun for me because the food was great, but the nurse only got to enjoy one scoopful of hummus because she immediately fled when her ex-boyfriend started crying and begging her to give him "one more chance, baby."

And, typical of my parents, they spun their failure into a success by congratulating each other for the next week and saying that "almost everyone had a *wonderful* time."

Except the actual person who was supposed to have a wonderful time!

I, too, have been a victim of my parents' horrible hobby. A few years ago, I made the mistake of telling my mom that I was sad Jeremiah Lavin hadn't invited me to his birthday bowling party. She said she'd "help cheer me up" by taking me bowling on the day of his party, but she wound up purposefully choosing the same bowling alley as the party. When we got there, she walked right up to Jeremiah and said, in a singsong voice, "Oh, Jeremiah. I think you forgot to invite someone." I didn't have time to hide before she pointed at me. Jeremiah just stared at me blankly. She gave me a hug, handed me a wrapped present, and whispered, "I'll come back to pick you up after the party. Have fun!" She winked at me and left. I wound up sitting by myself next to the rack of bowling shoes for the entire party and playing the electronic Uno game she had bought for me to give him.

My point is, if I told her anything about being gay, she'd want to know who I had a crush on; then she and my dad would pull one of their signature "helping out/scarring me for life" schemes.

"Becky?" she finally asked. "The girl?"

"Yes," I said, and offered nothing else. I figured the less information, the better. Let her and my dad hash out whether I was going through a phase. I went up to my room and tuned my violin.

After I squeaked my way through the Mendelssohn E

minor concerto (my favorite), I hightailed it to Spencer's house. I was so excited to tell him everything that had happened! Right when I turned onto his block, my phone vibrated.

I looked and I had an email from . . . CHUCK!

I couldn't believe he was already asking me out! I opened the email and, not surprisingly, he wasn't. BUT, he did write that he and Becky wanted to have dinner together and we should all meet at seven at the Japanese place in the mall.

Must. Control. Panting.

I'd never spent more than forty-five minutes (the length of a period at school) with him. This time, instead of being surrounded by other kids like we were at lunch today, it would be just him and me. (And Becky.) AH! This day was turning out to be the best of my life! I rang Spencer's doorbell, and as soon as he opened it, I got the apology out of the way.

"Spencer, I'm sorry I didn't sit with you and Mary Ann at lunch today."

He smiled and said, "That's OK."

I then stood back and waited for the "How did you get invited to sit at Cool U?" barrage of questions. Instead I got: "I'm going to make us something to drink," and he went into the kitchen.

Son of a—!

I was left in the foyer with an amazing story to tell and no audience! Where was the curiosity that had to have been consuming him all day? I walked into the kitchen with a hurt look and saw him making some chamomile tea.

"Oh, Justin, take off the sad face. I'm going to give you a chance to tell me how you got to sit with the so-called cool kids. I just felt I needed to be drinking something soothing while I listened." He brought our mugs to the kitchen table and took a deep breath. "Go."

I immediately launched into the whole story, and he was silent throughout it all. Hmm. I chose to believe that was because he was giving me his full attention and not because he was completely judging my conniving ways. Unfortunately, it was the latter.

"Justin," he said with a sigh after I finished my story and he finished his tea, "you have to know that this will never work out. A life manipulated is a life *something something*. Trying to force something to happen is like *blah blah blah*. The universe has a natural rhythm that *jibber jabber* . . ."

I successfully tuned out the bulk of what he was saying because I was not interested in him raining on my parade, even if that is my favorite song from *Funny Girl* (not the movie or *Glee* version—the original Broadway recording).

He then did what I knew he was going to do: He suggested that I skip meeting Chuck and Becky and instead do a meditation DVD with him. Oy! If it wasn't a DVD he was trying to get me to sit through, it was a book he wanted me to take home to read/do the exercises. FYI, any DVD that has a cover featuring a man with a white beard or any book that comes with a workbook should be avoided.

He saw my expression and tried to convince me.

"Meditation could be the key to finding out if you're following your true path."

He didn't get it! "I don't want to meditate, Spencer. I want to medi-*date* . . . Chuck!"

"Ow!" Spencer covered his ears. "That wasn't even a pun." I looked away, ashamed. "You see, Justin, even your amazing sense of humor is out of alignment because you're trying to alter nature's course."

That *was* a clunker, but I felt flattered he called my sense of humor amazing.

He looked at me intently. I thought about his reservations. No matter what, it was true that this Chuck/Becky charade *was* going to be life-altering. The only problem was, it could change my life for the better or, if Spencer was right, screw everything up because the universe doesn't like tricksters. Even though Spencer's New Age babbling often gave me a headache, I knew he had my best interests at heart. Maybe meditating on it would help me arrive at the right way to proceed. As well as give my face the attractive "at peace" look that Spencer often gets after an hour of chanting.

I sighed. "Put on the DVD." I figured I could watch the whole thing and still make the dinner date with Chuck. (And Becky.)

Spencer jumped up and turned on the brand-new TV he'd won in a raffle for the World Wildlife Fund.

I vowed to myself that this meditation DVD watching would be different. Normally, what would happen is this:

Spencer would talk me into watching a New Age DVD with him, I'd tell him to pause it for "just one minute" so I could tell him a quick story, and soon he'd forget about the DVD and wind up being my audience as my "quick story" segued into me lip-synching along with a Broadway CD. We sat cross-legged on his vegan rug, Spencer pushed PLAY, and the yogi began instructing us to breathe and clear our minds. After thirty seconds, I resisted the urge to tell Spencer who I think should host the Tony Awards this June (every Tony winner from the last ten years—how cool would that be?) and tried instead to focus on the yogi's instructions.

Clear my mind. Clear my mind. . . .

Pouting mouth, white-as-snow teeth . . .

AH! Clear my mind. Clear my mind. . . .

Piercing blue eyes, straight nose . . .

Clear it!

Sandy-blond longer-than-average hair . . .

Forget it. It was no use. I kept clearing, but Chuck kept infiltrating . . . and, quite frankly, I liked it! I didn't want to clear Chuck out of my mind. I wanted him there in residence. After ten minutes, I opened my eyes and caught a glimpse of myself in the glass of the cabinet that held the DVD player. Yowtch! I was decidedly unimpressed by what today's nervous sweat had done to my hair. I made an emergency decision to tiptoe out so I could sneak into the bathroom and use some of Spencer's mom's grooming supplies. I wanted to get my hair looking less 'fro before my Chuck encounter.

Let's see . . . open eyes, look slightly to left . . . now turn head . . . and . . . yes! Spencer looked to be completely out of it. Perfect.

I got up quietly and started sneaking toward the master bathroom.

Suddenly, I heard a voice that was not the yogi's.

"Justin, I know you're leaving."

Busted. I turned around.

He continued. "Just because I'm relaxed doesn't mean I'm in a coma." He had on his disappointed-grandfather face. "Listen." He got up and walked over to the TV and turned it off. "I wouldn't feel so strongly if I hadn't gone through the same thing with Mr. DelVecchio."

That again?

Mr. D, as everyone called him, was our ninth-grade English teacher. He was everyone's favorite teacher, but Spencer loved him in a "You're my teacher/father/best friend" sort of way. Mr. D had just graduated college and was *so* different from all the other teachers in school. He ate only locally grown food, played six-string guitar in a band, and was an actual pagan. Instead of assigning us written reports, he encouraged us to do videos, or PowerPoint presentations, or, in my case, musical numbers.

Mr. D was always willing to stay after school to talk about problems you were having in class or with other kids. It was great to have a teacher who was like a friend, but I think Spencer thought they actually *were* friends. It's not like Spencer had a crush on him; I just think he was a little needy because his dad had recently moved out. It must be hard having your parents not living together, and even though I tried to be supportive of what Spencer was going through, I couldn't really identify with him because my parents were happily married in a creepy sort of way (I actually once saw them kiss with tongue). Mr. D's parents were divorced or, as he said, "My old man split when I was ten," so Spencer liked talking with him.

Spencer joined the debate team that fall, even though it meant he had to quit his favorite after-school club, the math team. (Please don't get me started on how depressing it is that the math team is his favorite. It goes with my theory that every amazing person has one horrible, tragic flaw—for instance, Chuck hates the Twilight movies.) Spencer didn't like debating, but it meant he got to spend time with Mr. D after school.

One weekend in December, there was a big debate competition between our school and Chaminade Academy, which was two hours away. Spencer's dad was supposed to drive him, but he wound up having to stay home because his girlfriend's kid was sick, so Spencer's mom took him instead. When Spencer finally got to the tournament, Mr. D wasn't there. Spencer asked around and no one knew what had happened to him. Spencer didn't want to do the debate if Mr. D wasn't in the audience, but his mom had to go into work and wasn't coming back until the end of the day, so Spencer spent the whole tournament sitting in the boys' room of Chaminade, sending

Mr. D Facebook messages. Mr. D never wrote back, and on Monday we had a sub for English. Finally, that afternoon, Spencer found out that Mr. D's band got an offer to open for the Velvet Slashers and he had gone on tour. All the kids missed him, but Spencer was really upset. He was absent until that Thursday and didn't answer his cell phone whenever I called. It was actually the only time we went three days without talking.

"What does Mr. D flaking and going out on tour have to do with me and Chuck?"

"Because you're making the kind of mistake I made." I looked at him, confused. He went on. "I wanted to be Mr. D's friend so badly that I quit the math team."

"Yeah, the most amazing decision you ever made."

He shook his head, grandpa-style, and said, "The math team was me. Instead, I wound up being on the debate team and hating it and, after a few months, not even having Mr. D to coach me."

I looked at him and thought, *And????*

He sounded exasperated. "You're obsessed with Chuck. When someone wants something that badly, they make the wrong choices and it never works out."

He was so extreme. "What's wrong with wanting something a lot? It's called having a goal."

Spencer put on his "I'm going to teach you about life" face. "Justin, the Buddhist religion teaches us to renounce all worldly things."

"Chuck's not a worldly thing. He's a person." I then added, "And I'm not a Buddhist. I'm Jewish."

He shrugged. "One can be any religion, yet still practice the teachings of the Buddha."

All right. I'd had it. Enough already with his spirituality. I had a boyfriend to get.

"Listen, Spencer. I know you think I'm setting myself up for a big fat fall but *I* don't!" He looked like he was about to start listing how everything could blow up in my face, so I cut him off at the pass. "Let's make a deal. . . ."

I thought for a minute and continued. "I need around six months for my plan to come to fruition, so April will be the cutoff month."

Spencer nodded skeptically. "OK . . ."

"The deal is . . . we stay friends, but don't discuss the Chuck/Becky situation. If I'm not one of the happiest kids in school come April, I'll do a public dare."

Spencer and I are always making bets like this. Last year he'd had it with my Broadway babbling and (stupidly) bet me that I couldn't name all the Tony Award–winning best musicals for the last twenty years and, of course, I won. I made him do a public dare of trying out for the cheerleading squad. There was no gender specification on the posters announcing tryouts, but I knew he'd be the only guy in a sea of night-brace-wearing fourteen-year-old girls.

I was right, but unfortunately it backfired on me. The cheerleading coach thought Spencer was so good that the school has now formed an all-male squad and Spencer is the captain! Of course I'm dying to join, but I'm too angry to admit that my dare boomeranged in my face.

If Spencer lost this one, my public dare for him would have to be foolproof.

"Justin, how will I know if you're one of the happiest kids in school?"

Argh! Why must he always ask obvious questions? "My plan is to become one of the most popular kids. In the spring, you can ask the kids at school if they like me. If a majority of them say yes, I'm popular. Popular equals happy."

Spencer shook his head and started to speak, but I spoke first. "If I'm not on top of the world, you can make *me* do a public dare at"—I needed to sweeten the deal so he wouldn't keep undermining me for the next six months—"at the *Spring Fling*." The Spring Fling was the big dance that literally everybody in school attends. If you're gonna be publicly humiliated, that's a surefire way to make sure that no one has to hear about it secondhand.

Spencer looked like he was pondering everything. "There are too many holes in this. Let's say you become popular but aren't happy, but you say that you are just so you can make me do a public dare."

"Fine," I said. "You get to decide!"

"Meaning what?"

"Meaning you always know when I'm lying."

He immediately smirked. Every time I've tried to put one

over on him ("I haven't had sugar in a week!" "I think I may be bi"), he knew I was lying before I finished the sentence.

I continued. "If you think I'm happy, I win. If you think I'm not, you win."

He looked unconvinced. "I don't know if I approve of public dares anymore. It seems a little like I'm trying to control the universe. And, if I actually do win and come up with some way to humiliate you"—he looked like he was trying to find the right words—"it's as if I'm hoping to bruise your soul."

Bruise my soul? Why is everything such a big deal with him lately? Of course it's embarrassing when you lose a public dare, but that's the fun part! He was acting like we were planning a *Hunger Games*–style fight to the death.

I had to use all my lawyerly skills. "Spencer, it's not controlling the universe if we're *both* agreeing to enter a wager." He looked vaguely convinced. I went on. "And if you win, instead of trying to make the dare *bruise my soul*, like making me come to school in my underwear, you can make it"—I had to think of a phrase he would buy—"soothe my soul. Like . . . forcing me to go to a yoga retreat." Ironically, that would probably be more horrible for me than parading around in my underwear.

He thought about it for a moment, then put out his hand. "It's a deal," he said as I shook it.

I smiled. I felt sure I was gonna win. I looked at Spencer. He looked like *he* knew he was going to win . . . but didn't want to.

I LEFT SPENCER'S AND TOOK my time getting to the food court. I wanted to take in the anticipation of my first date with Chuck. (And Becky.) I arrived at the mall thirty minutes early and decided to make a pit stop at one of my favorite stores, The Body Shop. I first feigned looking at the men's stuff. I say "feign" because I never like the stuff they have for guys: It always smells like patchouli or other weird scents guys are supposed to like. After an appropriate amount of time elapsed (I could only take it for seven minutes), I then moved over to the ladies' stuff and picked up a sample bottle of moisturizer. In a volume I knew the salespeople could hear, I proclaimed, "Oh . . . I think my mom would like this dewberry lotion. Let me see what it smells like." I then proceeded to pour half the bottle on my arms and neck.

Mmm . . . delicious.

My next stop was The Nature Store, where I looked at

some cool books about weather. (I'm obsessed with hurricanes and tornadoes. Not the dying part, but the amazing winds and waves.)

Finally, it was time to go to the food court.

I had been waiting for one second when I saw Becky come up the escalator. I couldn't tell if she put on makeup for her date or if her whole face just naturally got more gorgeous because she knew she was going to meet Chuck. In my case, instead of naturally looking like I had a perfectly made-up face in anticipation of meeting Chuck, I naturally formed an extra layer of upper lip sweat. I quickly wiped it with the back of my sleeve.

"JUSTIN!" Becky screamed, and ran into my arms. She gave me a quick kiss on the lips and hugged me.

"Mmm," she said. "You smell so good!"

I smiled.

"Like my mother," she continued.

I stopped smiling.

Her reddish gold hair swung wildly as she did a 007-looking-for-spies move. She obviously decided the coast was clear because she started talking softly.

"I can't believe how well it worked. Everyone thinks we're a couple."

I gave her a thumbs-up. "You're the genius. And I guess your father deserves some thanks for surprising you yesterday."

"Oh!" she suddenly said. "That reminds me. I gotta call

him." She pulled her cell phone from a pink holder and pushed a speed-dial button.

"Hi, Daddy! I'm not gonna be home for din-din. I'm having Japanese." She paused. "Oh . . . Justin and some friends."

Pause.

"Yes, you can talk to him."

She handed the phone to me and put her hand over the receiver. "Don't worry. Just lie." Then she added, "I have to go to the bathroom. Be back soon!" And she walked off quickly, past the escalators.

"Hello?" I asked, not knowing where this was going to lead.

"Justin, my boy!" he said, with what can only be described as gusto. "I'm very glad you and my daughter seem so happy together."

Seem so happy together? He only saw us together yesterday for ten minutes. But I went with it.

"Oh, we are, Dr. Phillips!"

"Quite frankly, I'd love it if some of your bio skills could rub off on her."

"Ha, ha, ha, ha," I fake-laughed.

"Now, I know you also dabble in theater like she does. . . ."

Dabble? More like having a featured role in every show since fifth grade. I'm not counting my seventh-grade stint in the chorus, because I blame that on the phlegm attack I had during the audition due to Doug Gool's harassment of the afternoon, which consisted of forcing me into a toilet stall and smoking a pack of cigarettes in my face. "Well, it's a little more than dabbling . . . ," I began.

"That's because *you're* actually talented."

Wouch. PS, *wouch* is something Spencer and I made up, a combination of "wow" and "ouch." It was appropriate because I was both happy for the flattery and shocked that he'd dish about his daughter with me. And yet . . . he did have a point. Becky was always amazing in class or during rehearsals, but every time she performed in public with a chorus solo or a part in a show, she was ter-ri-ble. Sometimes she'd sing flat and sometimes she'd sing sharp. And mind-bogglingly, during one small solo in *Oklahoma,* her last note was flat *and* sharp, or "flarp" as I christened it with Spencer. Her other vocal "skill" was either no sound coming out of her mouth in the middle of a phrase or simply cracking . . . and not just on the high notes. She would crack on any note, no matter the range. She sang "Memory" when we did *Cats* at our synagogue's yearly Passover fund-raiser. Ouchy-wowy. I taped the whole show, and out of morbid curiosity, I listened to her again and again on my iPod for weeks afterward. I can offer a full analysis by heart:

(Music swells)

(flat) *Touch me!*

(forgets words) *to* (flat) *leave me!*

All alone with the (sharp) *mem'ry*

(inaudible) *of my days in the* (cracks) *sun.*

And whenever she did a show where she didn't have to

sing, her acting would be riveting in rehearsal but onstage she'd forget complete sections of dialogue. And the lines she did remember she would recite like a robot. It was maddening.

I was going to tell her dad that she actually has a lot of talent but needs to work on her performing skills. Unfortunately, he didn't give me a chance.

"Justin, listen. I have two tickets to the new musical at Lincoln Center. Are you interested?"

YES!!!!! I wanted to scream but didn't want to destroy Becky's cell phone with my loudness. I took a breath and said calmly, "Yes, sir. I am. That show is sold out for months."

He laughed. "I know. The producer's mom has been my patient for years. She offered me two tickets, and you were the first person I thought of."

Wow! Maybe he's not as bad as Becky thinks. "Thank you," I said, then added nervously, "Uh . . . when is it?" If it was two tickets, did that mean he'd be my "date" for the evening? Oy. It's awful enough to spend a night with your own father but devastating to spend it with someone else's.

"The first Saturday of next month. And don't worry, you can have both tickets."

Both tickets? Was there a catch?

"I just need you to do one thing. . . ."

Aha. I held the phone and waited for the perfunctory "Please respect my daughter's boundaries" speech he felt he had to say. I prepared for a five-minute stretch of time to tune him out and then I'd say a "yes, sir" as I came out of my stupor. Unfortunately, instead of the "my daughter is a delicate flower" oratory, I got "I need you to make sure Becky doesn't try out for *Rock and Roll High School.*"

What?

Background: *Rock and Roll High School* is the big musical coming up in April. Last year for the spring show, Mrs. Hall chose a Gilbert and Sullivan operetta that none of the theater kids had heard of. Everyone was so devastated that Mrs. H promised she would choose a show with a rock score for the next year if everyone stopped complaining before auditions even began. Well, she didn't quite phrase it like that. It was more: "If you kids promise to stop your yammering about hating a brilliant show, which, by the way, you know *nothing* about, I'll do one of those horrible high school pop shows next year. Now, all of you get on some antidepressants and shut the hell up." Of course, we wound up loving *H.M.S. Pinafore* because the music is fantastic and the lyrics are hilarious, but I'm glad we hated it at first because now we get to do a show where the lead role has to sing *and* play the piano.

YES! Who else at our school can sing and really play the piano?

And Zelda Chung doesn't count because the role is for a boy. But there are amazing parts for girls, too. If Becky got over her performance awfulness, she'd be perfect for the cheer-leader lead.

I didn't know what to say to Becky's dad. I wanted those

tickets. But wouldn't it be wrong to make Becky not audition? I mean, it's true I'd be saving her the embarrassment of a bad performance because that's probably what would happen. Wait a minute . . . the more I think about it, the more I feel I'd actually be doing her a favor.

No, you wouldn't. You'd be using her in order to get a material possession you want.

AH! I not only have to deal with Spencer in real life but also in my head? That area is reserved solely for Chuck.

I saw Becky walking back from the bathroom.

"Oh, here comes Becky now," I said. "I'll be sure to talk to her," I added, without specifying what I'd be talking to her about.

"Good boy!" he said to me . . . or possibly to his dog. "I'll hold those tickets for you."

"Thanks!" I said.

As I was about to hand the phone back to Becky, he added, "If."

That's all he said. Literally "If" followed by a period. Hmph. Not only was that vaguely threatening, but it's also a sentence fragment. Hadn't he ever taken Mr. Fabry's English grammar intensive?

Becky took the phone and said bye and a perfunctory "I love you" to him.

We started to walk toward Sushi Yummy. "What did he want to talk to you about?" she asked, and her catlike eyes looked so innocent. Oh no. I hadn't had enough time to work out a lie.

"Um . . . ," I started.

She smirked. "Probably asking you to help me get into AP bio . . ."

"YES!" I said, much too loudly, grateful that she thought of the lie for me. "I can do flash cards with you if you want."

She looked annoyed. "I don't want. *He* wants."

She started getting in line and I looked around. Where was Chuck?

"Um . . . Becky. Aren't we supposed to wait for Chuck?"

"Oh," she said while getting her tray, "don't worry. He always comes late. Either practice goes over or he decides to spend an extra half hour on the treadmill."

That's annoying. But, frankly, he's worth waiting for.

Becky saw me hesitating by the trays. "Don't wait for him." I got my tray and we started moving past all the delicious sushi choices. "The sad part is, he might have eaten already. He's always shoveling protein bars down his gut and calling it a meal."

Protein bars? So *that's* how he stays so muscular. Well, muscular and lean. Not too muscley. Just the right amount. His biceps don't necessarily bulge, they—

"What do you look so happy about?" Becky suddenly asked.

Caught!

I said the first thing I could think of.

"Eel rolls!"

"You're in luck!" she said with a beautiful smile. "They have them."

I know. I saw them near the California rolls.

"Here." She put three on my plate.

Great. The first thing that came to me was eel rolls but not because I love them; they were on my mind because I hate them. UCK. Eels are so ugly. They look like creatures from hell. That sushi recipe is like cutting up evil and serving it rolled in rice.

Of course, they're more expensive than other rolls, so I only had enough money left over for a side salad. Becky and I sat down at one of the food court tables with umbrellas, and I chose the side where I could see the escalator Chuck would have to take.

Becky and I started eating (delicious sushi for her and lettuce for me).

We chewed.

No sign of Chuck.

We swallowed.

Was that Chuck on the escalator?

No . . .

"So . . . ," she said.

"So, yeah," I said.

What now? We knew each other from various rehearsals

but hadn't ever spent any time alone. Except for the recent morning walk to school, and that was more of a planning session. What could we talk about? The only thing I could think of was her father's scheme, and I couldn't bear the thought of carrying it out. I tried to force it out of my mind so I wouldn't have to deal with it.

"Becky, are you trying out for *Rock and Roll High School*?"

Great. I forced it out of my mind, right into my mouth.

"Oh!" she said excitedly. "I need to ask you something about that."

Well, the good news was we had something to talk about; the bad news was it was something I didn't want to talk about.

"Lots of people don't try out," I said, which related to nothing she'd said.

Thankfully, at that moment her cell phone rang.

She looked at the screen. "It's Chuck!" She flipped her hair back and answered it. "Hi, honey." She listened for a while, nodding.

"OK," she finally said. "See you then."

Phew. At least he'd given an estimated time of arrival.

"How late is he gonna be?" I asked, trying to make it sound like I was frustrated because it was an inconvenience for me to have to wait for them to have their date and not because I'd expected to see Chuck's stunningness and now had to wait.

"Oh, he's not coming."

WHAT?

She went on. "It's like I thought. Practice went on longer and now he wants to hit the treadmill and then stretch. I'm going to see him tomorrow morning in geometry."

Excellent. I left Spencer's so I could eat a side of greens and stare at a plateful of food that made me gag.

Becky put her phone into her bag. "Let's talk about the spring show."

And be forced to have a conversation I would do anything to avoid.

What an amazing first date with Chuck.

8

THAT ALL HAPPENED TWO WEEKS ago.

I'm now in my Monday study hall. Usually I spend the period quietly sitting and studying, which usually deteriorates into me fantasizing about starring opposite Kristin Chenoweth in a Broadway musical that's filmed for TV and then gets released as a major motion picture. Instead, I've spent the whole period today passing notes. And not like I used to, which was like this:

1. One of the cool kids would write a note.

2. They'd slip it to me while whispering to whom to pass it.

3. They'd then tell me NOT to open it.

4. I'd pass it to a cool kid and risk getting in trouble.

5. Repeat from opposite direction.

This time they didn't want me to pass it to anyone; instead it was being passed to *me*! The notes were mostly making fun of E.R.'s (Ms. Horvath's) neck brace. She apparently fell off the treadmill she has to walk on, according to doctor's orders, "every day for twenty *full* minutes." She had been complaining about her regimen for weeks: "It's supposed to be physical therapy, but it's physical *agony*." She informed us that last week she hadn't been able to take the "torture" anymore, so she'd pushed the STOP button. Apparently the treadmill didn't slow gradually; it just stopped and the abruptness of it made her neck snap "all the way forward and all the way back." She told anyone who walked by that she now had "fifth-degree whiplash."

First of all, I didn't know whiplash came in degrees, and secondly, when things *are* registered in degrees, don't they only go up to third? Also, is fifth degree the worst level or is it at the low end of the spectrum? No one dares ask her for fear of the personal medical history we'll have to endure. Regardless, her injury has been the subject of most of the notes today, featuring pictures of her with arrows pointing to various body parts. Next to the arrows were written things like "seventh-degree halitosis" and "twelfth-degree hemorrhoid" (that was mine).

Usually when I looked around a classroom, my view would be mainly kids I wasn't allowed to talk to (too cool) and kids I was too scared to talk to (too tough). But now, thanks to Becky, I can talk to *any* of the cool kids. Yes, it's still for limited amounts of time (aka until someone cooler comes along and I get dropped), but it's more words than I've spoken to them in fifteen years! AND now the tough kids don't call me fag, etc., anymore because my girlfriend is so "hot."

Even Doug Gool stopped actively bothering me. Oddly enough, though, he's stepped up his harassment of Mary Ann Cortale. It seems that ever since he put chocolate on her butt, he's taken all the hatred he had toward me and directed it toward her. Whenever I'm at my locker, he's in front of hers in the middle of writing *skank* or gluing her lock or taping up rolls of toilet paper. I feel bad that she's bearing the brunt of him, but I can't really do anything about it; plus I have too much other stuff to deal with.

My main issue is trying to get all my homework done and piano/violin practicing in while still having time every day for a Chuck-and-Becky rendezvous. I've started to wake up extra early so I can get my practicing done in the morning, because after school I have to be on call. So far I haven't been able to work a whole lot on getting Chuck interested in me because we haven't spent much time together. Normally what happens is I'll get a last-minute phone call to meet at a location where I'll show up early and meet Becky. We chat until Chuck shows up (at least twenty minutes late, sometimes up to an hour); then they'll go off somewhere and make out while I keep a lookout. Also, in the last week alone, he's canceled three times because of practice/the gym/the coach/the team. It's not exactly what I'd envisioned, but at least it's gotten me one item I can cross off my goals-for-the-year list: school-wide popularity. Well, not exactly popularity, but no one's being mean to my face.

Therefore, the next step is figuring out a way to amp up my popularity. Yes, kids don't actively ignore/hate me, and they chat with me before and after class, but where are the invitations to parties? Where are the late-night, two-hour phone calls? Where are the bare-your-soul conversations while you walk through the park? In other words, where's all the stuff I get from Spencer? I won't feel truly popular until one of the cool kids calls me and we spend an hour watching a reality show together while on the phone. I'm trying to figure out what I need to do to make that happen since it seems that dating Becky and being funny aren't enough to get to that next level. *And* while I'm figuring that out, I have to work on the other two items on my sophomore-year list: dating Chuck and getting my first kiss!

The unexpected thing I'm having to deal with as well is Becky and *Rock and Roll High School.* When we were at the mall eating Japanese food (aka a side salad for me), she asked me if she could come to my house in a few weeks so I could work with her on her audition. Unfortunately, the day we decided to meet is today. Oh yeah, since I play the piano, I sometimes help people get their audition songs into shape. Normally I'd be super-excited to help Becky because I think she's really talented and I love telling someone how to sing a song . . . I mean, *suggesting* to someone how to sing a song. The problem is her father. If I help her audition, I won't get those tickets to the Lincoln Center show. For the past two weeks, I've been trying to think of a great excuse to keep her from coming over, like "My mom has a migraine," "My piano broke," and, I'm ashamed to admit, "I have fifth-degree whiplash." Finally, this morning I was going to pull the old stomach flu routine, but before I could, she told me she was sick of Chuck being late or sometimes not even showing up, so she told him he *had* to come this afternoon. How could I pass up a chance to have Chuck in my house?! Maybe they'll come over and we'll all wind up chatting for so long that we never get around to working on her audition and I'll still be able to snag those Lincoln Center tickets. Or maybe her dad will call her on her cell and she'll have to leave earlier than Chuck and he'll wind up staying for dinner. Or a snack. Or a severe make-out session.

Oops. I have to pass a note!

OK, so this afternoon around four, Chuck and Becky arrived within minutes of each other. I wanted a good hour to gaze at Chuck so I could memorize what his blond stunningness looks like in my house and replay it over and over again in my mind for years to come. Instead, Becky immediately took out her audition song and put it on my piano. I was about to feign arthritis in my hands, but Chuck suddenly looked over and said, "Hey, Justin. I didn't know you played." ARGH! That's what drives me crazy about this school. I've played and sung in *every* chorus concert and *all* the musicals, and I know the cool kids would be impressed if they heard me in action, but the only people who come to those performances are the parents of the kids performing. Or a handful of kids who aren't performing but love the arts and are therefore in a low social echelon. I wish that attendance at the plays and chorus concerts was mandatory for every kid in school. Hearing me sing a solo with an entire chorus behind me or belt out a big song and dance number in a musical would be just the thing to get me to the real popularity level I want to be at.

Chuck sat right next to me. "C'mon, Justin, play something."

Mmm . . . He'd obviously just been chewing gum because I was enveloped in a cloud of Doublemint. My vision began to blur and I started to play the only thing I could think of: the music in front of me. Becky took that as a cue that her coaching session with me had started and began singing. Hmph. So much for me not helping her. The cheerleader in *Rock and Roll High School* has a big song in the second act that she sings to the freshman character. The theme is "I've been where you are and this is what I've learned. Don't make the same mistakes I did." Since the song has an old-school R & B/pop feel to it, Becky decided to sing a 1980s Whitney Houston classic. "The Greatest Love of All" was Whitney's first big hit and has a similar theme to the cheerleader's song in the show. It also has some super-high notes that are impossible for most people to sing. Becky sang the whole song without any of her onstage issues: no flat/sharpness, memory loss, inappropriate softness, or cracking. After she finished her final "*lo-o-o-o-o-o-ve!*" I was speechless. She belted *all* the high notes and even added some sassy riffs she made up. *Plus* her acting choices were amazing. It's like she stopped being Becky and had this inner glow that conveyed power and wisdom yet some kind of past hardship she didn't want anyone else to go through, just like the character. Chuck started clapping. I was waiting for Becky to acknowledge him, but I turned and saw he was clapping toward *me!*

"Wow, Justin. You got talent." He caressed my shoulder. Well, more like he patted me on the back. Well, not really patted, more like he *pat* me on the back. Hmm. I think he was just using my back for leverage as he got up, but nevertheless, there was touching involved.

Still, I couldn't believe he was impressed by that. That's not even a hard song to play. *Wait until he hears me play the Chopin scherzo in F sharp minor,* I thought. I then decided I should probably stick to playing Whitney. That kind of music is more impressive to people like Chuck. And anyone under seventy-five.

I thanked him and was waiting for him to go even crazier for Becky. If he was praising *me* that much, I knew he was going to go overboard for her because she really sounded amazing!

Instead, he got up and started dialing his phone. "I gotta

call the coach," he said as he walked out of the room. "If we're gonna practice outside this winter, the hot chocolate machine better get fixed."

Chuck went into the kitchen and I looked at Becky. She had lost all of the glow she had during the song and was now looking down. How could she be depressed after such an amazing performance? I had to tell her how great she was.

"Becky!" I said, and she looked up. "That was incredible!" She had to know that. I decided to get a little nitpicky. "My only advice about auditioning with that song would be to—"

"Oh, Justin, what does it matter?" She flopped down on the couch.

Huh? What was she being such a downer about? "Listen, Becky, I don't know why Chuck didn't tell you how gorgeous you sounded, but—"

She laughed. "Oh, please. Chuck never says anything about the way I sing. Or look. Or . . . anything. That's just Chuck."

Hmm. That sounds annoying. But I could certainly deal with it just to have one delicious hour wrapped in his muscular—

"I've gotten used to Chuck." Becky broke me out of my mini-fantasy. "That's not why I'm upset."

"Well, do you think it's the wrong song choice? I think it's great, but if you don't"—I started flipping through papers on my piano—"I have the music here somewhere. Maybe you can learn a song from the show."

"Justin. I've been listening to the CD all year. I have every song memorized. That's not the issue."

"Then what's up?" I asked, and walked over to where she was sitting on the couch.

She sighed. "I was feeling so good about the song and my chances for getting cast—"

"Exactly!" I interrupted. "You *have* to get the cheerleader part. No one else in the school can sing like you."

"That's what I was thinking . . . then I saw *this*." She held up a picture of the cast of *Cats*. Not the Broadway musical, but the one we did at synagogue. There in the front row was me (in a full split) as Old Deuteronomy and right in back (next to the rabbi's wife, who was a sixty-year-old Jennyanydots) was Becky, working her natural green cat eyes in her Grizabella catsuit.

She brandished the photo in its frame. "I'm dreading another horrible performance."

"Oh, stop it, Becky. You weren't horrible," I lied.

"Yes, I was. My version of 'Memory' stank." Then she breathed a sigh of relief. "I'm just thankful it wasn't recorded."

Note to self: delete bootleg of synagogue Cats *performance from iPod.*

"Well, stop worrying. Your voice sounds incredible now."

"Justin," she said with her hands on her hips. "Didn't I sound incredible in *Cats* rehearsal?"

"Yeah . . . ," I said tentatively.

"Don't I sound great at *all* rehearsals?"

"Yes, you do," I said, dreading what was coming.

"OK. Now name me one *performance* in which I've sounded incredible."

Ouch.

"Um . . ."

Must. Fill. Silence.

"Well, Becky, there was that concert . . . that time . . . during the . . . thing. . . ." I nodded like I had just completed a coherent sentence.

"Forget it, Justin. I have ears. I know that every time I get in front of an audience, I suck."

She was right. But obviously she had a great voice. If she always panicked during performances and lost all of her vocal talent, there had to be some reason for it.

"I'm *not* going to audition," she said firmly.

True, there had to be some reason for it, but why find out? Lincoln Center, here I come!

"Um . . . are you sure?" I forced myself to ask. I did this mostly to placate Spencer, who I knew was going to go over this exchange with a fine-tooth comb searching for my karma.

"Yes, I'm sure," she said, taking the Whitney music off the piano and sending my heart soaring. "I came here today in denial. You can tell Chuck I went home."

And with that, she went out the front door.

And left Chuck.

Alone.

In my HOUSE!

He walked into the living room. *Here's my chance*, I thought. I took a deep breath and—

He looked around. "Did Becky leave?"

"Well, Chuck, I think she did. Perhaps you and I—"

"Oh, man," he interrupted. "She was supposed to pay me back the ten bucks she owed me."

I didn't know what to say. "That's too bad . . . ," I offered.

He looked crestfallen. "That's exactly how much more money I need to be able to buy those new sneakers. You know, the ones with the double air cushions."

I didn't know anything about sports sneakers, but I did know he looked adorable when he was sad.

"Justin, would you"—he moved closer—"could you . . ." He was right in front of my face. I could have reached out with my lips and touched his. He suddenly moved away. "Nah . . . I couldn't ask you to lend me money."

Yes, he could, if it meant he would come that close again!

"Chuck, it's no problem." I ran to get my wallet.

One minute later, I handed him a twenty-dollar bill.

"That's all I have," I explained. "Do you—"

Before I could ask him for change, he yelled, "You're the best!" and grabbed his coat. "Thanks, Justin. I'm hittin' the mall!"

He waved and ran out my front door.

I stood and thought about his powerful leg muscles propelling him to the mall.

Well, propelling him to the shuttle bus that stopped at my corner and would take him to the mall.

I took a deep breath.

Wow.

I just experienced Chuck flirting with me.

Things are moving along as planned.

And I'm going to the Lincoln Center show.

Things are even better than I expected!

Right?

9

THE LINCOLN CENTER SHOW WAS A-MA-ZING! I'm about to go to sleep because I had to spend the last hour obsessively reading through the *Playbill* over and over again and now it's super-late, but here's the backstory quickly. When I first knew I was definitely going to the show, I desperately wanted to give Chuck the other ticket, but I was smart enough not to ask him. Yes, I'm working toward dating/smooching him, but even *I* know that when we're dating, there'll be no afternoons in Manhattan, having brunch and taking in a musical. That's why I have Spencer. He's not even into Broadway like I am, but he's always willing to come along with me whenever I want to see a show, and because he's so smart, he'll always have something incredibly insightful to say about it afterward.

My mom dropped us off at the Long Island Rail Road. "Have fun!" she said as we got out of the car. We started walking up the stairs, and she leaned out the window.

"Justin! Don't you have to wait down here for Becky?"

Ugh! Lately she's been asking me all the time how things are going with Becky and if she wants to come over to our house for dinner. I know she's trying to figure out what's really going on, and it takes so much effort to keep giving vague answers so she and my dad will keep out of it. This time, because we were halfway up the stairs, I had the advantage of distance.

"Peas and carrots, peas and carrots!" I yelled. We had learned in Mrs. Hall's theater class that when you're in a crowd scene and you're supposed to make general crowd noises, just repeat "Peas and carrots" and it does the trick. And, from a distance, it looks like you're saying something.

"What?" she yelled as the car behind her started to honk.

That was my cue. I gave her a thumbs-up and pulled Spencer up the stairs. I promptly turned off my cell phone so she couldn't ask any further questions, and Spencer and I stood on the platform, waiting for the train.

"Your mother still doesn't know your devious plan?"

"No," I replied. Then added, "And it's not devious."

Spencer did his "no response" routine, which I knew was a way to make me examine what I just said. But I took it as a cue to talk about global warming. I knew if I mentioned something he was interested in, he'd get his mind off me and Chuck and Becky.

Right when he was talking about the long-term effects of the Gulf of Mexico oil spill, the train arrived. As we were getting on, I noticed that he looked adorable. Underneath his overcoat, he was wearing a casual brown blazer that contrasted with his orange hair perfectly. I mentioned how much I loved his coat, and he told me he got it at a Housing Works thrift store, which gives all their profits to help homeless people with AIDS. Leave it to Spencer to figure out a way to look good while saving the world.

When we arrived at Penn Station, we decided to have brunch on the Upper West Side because Lincoln Center is in the West 60s. Spencer found a place that looked great called Nice Matin, and we actually got a table by the window. Last week we had a late-November snow, and my mom gave me some cash for shoveling, so I told Spencer I was treating him to the meal.

After Spencer got his orange juice, he raised it to his lips, then stopped, pre-sip.

"Justin, just confirm for me that I'm not drinking orange juice paid for with blood money."

UGH! "You are not, Spencer." Everything with him was at such an extreme level lately. "That money is from my mom. And besides, Becky decided not to audition for the show without any influence from me."

Spencer took a tentative sip.

"You may have forgotten," I went on, trying to will him to finish the glass, "but all I did was tell her how great she sounded."

Spencer nodded thoughtfully. "I know, I know. You told

me. I just don't like that you were paid off by her father. Even if you didn't do what he wanted."

I rolled my eyes. How many times did we have to go over this?

"All right, Justin." He took one more sip. "I'm going to have brunch and see the show with you, and I promise not to be a 'moral downer' all day, as I know you've called me in the past"—*I've said that out loud?*—"but I've thought about the whole Becky-audition thing, and I've come to the conclusion that what you've done is the equivalent of lying by omission."

"Meaning?" I asked, but it came out as "Mmgtmgnidn" because I was eating one of the delicious croissants that arrived in a bread basket before the meal.

"Meaning, which I think you just said, that you could have spent some time with her figuring out why she isn't up to snuff when she performs."

"Not 'up to snuff'? She's stinks," I clarified.

"Exactly. And it isn't because she doesn't have talent. That girl belongs onstage, just like you do, and yet you let her decide not to audition without any argument."

"Well," I said, and then took time to swallow, "it's too late now. Pamela Austin has the role."

The auditions happened at the beginning of this week and, not surprisingly, I got the lead! Finally, there was a show with a leading role where the requirement wasn't being great-looking. I've gotten sick of playing the sassy sidekick, and I've always wanted the experience of taking the final bow.

Unfortunately, once Becky was out of the running, Pamela was the best singer out of all the kids auditioning. This year, as usual, only a smattering of kids tried out because Mrs. Hall requires that students take theater class if they want to be in the big show. Even though *Glee* has suddenly made my whole school want to sing and dance, hardly anyone wants to actually train, so there were slim pickin's at the audition. Pamela doesn't have Becky's acting talent or amazing high notes or phenomenal riffs but . . . she can sing. Not like a rock, pop, or R & B singer, but the only other girls who auditioned and could actually sing or look the part were Nell Malin, who has an amazing voice . . . on operatic songs; Mary Ann Cortale, who didn't prepare an audition song so she sang "Happy Birthday" *and* forgot the words; and Zelda Chung, whose parents won't let her sing anything "immoral," so all the lyrics in the show would have to be changed to be about God. None of the other girls could ever pass for a cheerleader, and the whole point of the role is to show that although she's beautiful on the outside, she's sad on the inside.

When Pamela arrived on the first day of rehearsal, Mrs. Hall mentioned that it might be hard to do all the cheerleading moves in the show with her hair hanging to her waist, so perhaps she could wear it up. That led to Pamela bursting into tears and claiming, "I've worn my hair this way my whole life" and then fleeing and locking herself in a bathroom stall. Unfortunately, she ran to the first bathroom she saw, which was the boys, and I had just drunk a full liter of diet Snapple.

Suffice it to say, I was very uncomfortable using the urinal two feet away from Pamela's sobbing, and I gave new meaning to the term *shy bladder* (estimated peeing time: seven minutes).

Spencer asked me how things with Chuck were progressing, and I said "fine" without being specific. I didn't want to mention the flirting thing because if I did, I'd have to mention that he still hadn't paid me back the twenty dollars. Then Spencer would say he was only flirting to get cash out of me, and I was not in the mood to start arguing about that. I was there and I know Chuck *was* flirting with me. The money part was secondary.

Thankfully, Spencer and I wound up having a great time. I've hardly spent any time with him since the aborted meditation session because I've been so busy with Becky and Chuck. I'm still adjusting my personality with the cool kids to try to rise even higher in popularity, and it was a pleasure to just be myself with Spencer, even if it was only for an afternoon. I ordered a goat cheese egg-white omelet and was waiting for Spencer to order his signature bacon "very, very, very well done," but he only got the fresh herb omelet with no sides.

I stared, dumbfounded, after we ordered. "Spencer! Where's the delish bacon? I'm the one on the diet." I finally started a diet because when I do eventually wind up with Chuck, I don't want people to look at our prom picture and think, *Why is he with* him? (I'm *him*.)

"Oh yeah," Spencer said, looking a little embarrassed. "I'm sort of experimenting with being kosher."

"What?" I yelled, resulting in getting glared at by the James Gandolfini look-alike at the next table, whom I then realized was a woman. Yowtch. "You're not even Jewish! Why would you adopt the part of the religion that's the most annoying to follow?"

He shrugged. "I'm just trying different things." Spencer has always been spiritual/respect the earth, but this year he was a combination Mother Teresa/Gandhi/Dalai Lama, and now Tevye. The rest of the afternoon was super-fun. We walked to the theater and at one point we laughed for five blocks straight. I can always make him laugh but then he'll top what I say and make us both laugh hysterically.

Speaking of laughing, I finally made Chuck laugh! Until I slim down a little bit, I've got to lure him with whatever attractiveness I've got, and my sense of humor doesn't have love handles. I met up with Becky and him at the gazebo by Goose Pond. It's got a great view of the water, and in the winter they cover it to keep in the warmth, but it's still pretty cold. Hence, we knew we'd be the only ones there.

Chuck was, as usual, on the phone for a while and Becky started coughing, perhaps because it was thirty degrees outside the gazebo and thirty-five inside.

"Becky!" he said after he hung up. "You cough so loud! Man . . ." He shook his head. "I could hardly hear the coach."

Becky didn't respond, so I tried to break the tension.

"Well," I said, "it's better than coughing like Monsieur Bissel." I then did my imitation of our French teacher's cough, which wasn't so much about the sound but about the crazy physicality. If he's about to have one of his smoker's hack fits, he'll always grab on to something to steady himself, put one hand daintily on his throat, and then for some reason, clamp his eyes shut during every cough. I did a few and Chuck couldn't stop laughing. "Dude!" he said. "You look just like him!"

I felt so triumphant making him laugh. I was about to launch into it again when he turned to Becky and said, "And you look hot!" and they started making out. Hmph.

I spent their make-out time thinking about how close Chuck had been to my face at my house. Ah . . .

I don't know how long my trance lasted, but it ended right when their make-out session did. It was freezing and I wanted to get a delicious hot chocolate on my way home, but my wallet was depressingly empty. I thought maybe Chuck would have at least ten of the twenty dollars I'd lent him; but right when I was about to ask him, he looked at me and said, "Justin, man, you are wicked funny." First, the brazen flirting and now the appreciation of my humor. Who cared about the twenty bucks?! I wore such a look of love that I was scared Becky would pick up on my master plan. Ah! I had to erase it from my face! I thought of peeing near Pamela Austin in the boys' room, and I immediately looked disgusted.

Chuck lived in the opposite direction and made a hasty exit. It was now my job to walk Becky home. She and I walked out of the gazebo and toward her house. Oy. What to talk about?

"So . . . that was a pretty long make-out session." *That's* my version of conversation? No wonder the popular kids still don't want to be my best friend.

"You're right," Becky said with a little smile. "I think a part of me is trying to re-create the first time, you know?"

I actually didn't know. "First time what?"

"You know . . . my first kiss." She closed her eyes. "Mmm, I'll never forget what it was like."

Now I was interested. "What was it like?" I asked, hoping for the kind of details I could retain and later think about with my face in the place of Becky's.

"Well"—she opened her eyes and pushed some of her red-dish gold hair into her wool hat—"Chuck and I had been flirting at lunch for a few months but he never asked me out." I knew what that was like. Without the flirting-at-lunch part. "Finally, we were at one of Michelle Edelton's parties." She laughed. "You know how crazy those get!"

My face said, "Yes, I do" while my brain said, "No, I don't."

Becky stopped to pick up a handful of snow and then threw it into the air. "Everyone was dancing and Chuck suddenly walked up to me and asked if I wanted to leave. I nodded."

Perfect, the fewer words she said in the situation, the easier it will be to imagine it's me later on.

She continued. "Instead of going out the front door, we went out the back and found ourselves in her garden. No one else was there." She looked away dreamily. "Michelle has this bench right next to a big rosebush and we sat on it. He still didn't ask me out, but he took my face in his hands and leaned forward and then . . . we kissed." She closed her eyes again.

So did I. When I opened mine, she still had hers closed.

"So, that was your first kiss?"

"Yes." She turned toward me, and her eyes sparkled. "You never forget it, right?"

I smiled and pretended to remember mine. "That's right," I parroted back. "You never forget it."

She shivered. "That tingly feeling of excitement and happiness. It goes all through your body." She sighed. "It's like no other feeling."

So *that's* what it's gonna be like.

Thankfully she didn't ask for details of mine or I would have had to do some creative babbling.

We kept walking.

We were both thinking about kissing Chuck.

We turned onto her block. She looked thoughtful. "He was almost a different person back then. He hadn't made quarterback yet, and he hadn't hit that home run in the last baseball game of the spring. . . ." She trailed off.

What did she mean? That he was an even *more* amazing catch now? 'Cause that's what I was thinking.

Becky hugged me on her porch. "Bye, Justin," she said

while taking out her keys. Then she looked at me with a half smile. "It's always so great to talk to you."

She walked into her house. I stood there. One of the most popular girls in school just told me how great it is to talk to me. Annoyingly, I didn't feel as happy as I thought I would. It's probably because I need a bunch of the popular kids to really like me before I truly feel fantastic. Having Becky like me is similar to having a fresh new dollar bill. It's certainly nice, but it's much nicer to have a *million* fresh new dollar bills. Or at least however many kids sit at Cool U.

FINALLY! CHRISTMAS VACATION! I NEEDED a break. I'd had it with the nonstop homework. Well, my own homework and the extra homework I was obligated to do. You see, around three weeks ago, I was waiting for Chuck and Becky at the mall and it was one of the rare times that Chuck got there before Becky. I was, of course, speechless seeing him but luckily he started talking right away.

"We got out of practice early because some doofus broke his arm when I tackled him."

I decided to pretend that Chuck sounded sympathetic. "That's too bad."

Silence.

How could I make him go back to the flirting? And maybe take it further?

I added, "Becky's not here," awkwardly stating the obvious.

"I know," he said with a sudden smile. "Which is perfect."

Perfect? Yes. Perfect for me! But why for him?

He put his arm around me. It was in a "we're both dudes" way, but it was the closest I'd ever been to him. My breathing suddenly accelerated as if I had run for a half hour on the treadmill. And I basically can't breathe after just fifteen minutes of fast walking.

"Justin, dude . . . " I could feel his breath on my neck. Heaven. "Do you mind helping me out a little with French homework? I didn't want to ask you in front of Becky."

"Help you out? No problem!" I answered right away. I'd *love* to tutor him. I could come to his house. Sit with him in his room. It could get late. He'd ask me to sleep over and then . . . it could work out better than I ever expected.

But I didn't understand why he didn't want to ask in front of Becky.

He then handed me his French take-home quiz.

"I already signed it," he said as he pointed to the honor pledge at the end promising that he hadn't cheated. "You can just fold it up and slip it into my locker tomorrow."

Oh.

He wasn't asking me to "help" him with his homework; he wanted me to "do" his homework. *That's* why he didn't want Becky to know. I remembered hearing that Becky found out last year that he had bought a research paper from someone he met online and she forced him to throw it out and write it himself. She was a stickler for honesty. Except, of course, when it came to her dating life.

I thought about it. Do his homework for him? Hmm. Unfortunately, Spencer had rubbed off on me throughout the years, and I, too, would never consider cheating on anything. I made my decision. Even though I wanted Chuck to be the Edward to my Bella, I had to say no. But before I did, he looked me right in the eye, just like he had at my house, and said, "Please, Justin."

Then . . . he winked! It wasn't just a "dude" wink. It reeked of sexiness. Suddenly, we both heard Becky shout us out a big hello from near the Gap. She was walking to meet us, and Chuck grabbed his homework, shoved it at me, and said, "Quick, before she gets here!" I was about to weakly protest when he whispered, "Justin. You know I think you're the best."

That's all it took. I grabbed the homework and put it into my bag. Now we have a ritual that after French class, he walks out right behind me and slips the homework into my backpack. Then I do it and slip it into his locker right after study hall. I just have to copy all the answers I write down in my version of his handwriting. It's not that hard . . . and you should have seen the sexiness of that wink. It plays in my mind more times than Hannah Montana reruns on the Disney Channel.

This whole vacation week I pretty much vegged out at my house. My mom didn't ask me how my dates with Becky were going because she knew Becky was off skiing with her family. Unfortunately, I didn't get any private Chuck time because he was with his parents in New Hampshire where they have a house. There aren't a lot of Christmas parties in my school, since the majority of the kids are Jewish.

But New Year's Eve is a BIG deal, and if you're not actually having a party, you're invited to one. My parents, however, are the exception. They always spend New Year's Eve having what they call a romantic dinner with dancing in Manhattan. They took a semester of ballroom dancing in college together, and this is the one night a year where they use their skills (not counting weddings and Bar Mitzvahs). They go out to some fancy restaurant that has a big band and, according to them, spend the night making everyone jealous of their moves. Since it's their yearly "night to reconnect," I'm never invited.

I had a babysitter up until fifth grade, but after that I've spent every New Year's Eve at Spencer's house. We order in pizza and then at eight o'clock we play a board game. However, it's never something like Uno or Battleship. We want it to be something that will take hours to play and keep us up until midnight. At first it was Risk, but for the past four years it's been Monopoly. Not everyday Monopoly and not any of the themed ones you can buy, like The Wizard of Oz or New York or something horrible like sports. Instead, we make it themed with stuff related to us! Last year I was in charge and designed one all about school lunches. My playing piece was a miniature lunch tray and Spencer's was a tiny lunch plate with a meticulously placed hair glued across it (Spencer once got a plate with a hair on it and returned it, horrified, and then the next one *also* had a hair on it!). I turned all properties into meals—aka expensive Boardwalk and Park Place became Cheese Quesadillas and Caesar Salad (our favorites) and cheap Baltic Avenue became Tuna Fish (the most disgusting). Instead of "Go to Jail" cards, it was "Sit at Toughs 'R' Us" (Doug Gool's table), and when you passed GO, you collected 200 calories. The goal was to have the most calories and become morbidly obese.

This year was Spencer's turn to make the Monopoly game. I went over to his place at six, we ordered our signature pizza (double-cheese Sicilian), and he unveiled the game. He told me it was dedicated to me and then ceremonially took off the towel lying across it. It was Broadway-themed! Yay! He showed me my playing piece, which was a mini Evita with arms raised Patti LuPone–style, and his was Tracy Turnblad from *Hairspray*. He doesn't know that much about Broadway, but he obviously did his research. Every property was a different Broadway show, and instead of "Go to Jail" it was "Go on a Non-Union Tour." Inwardly, I was sad that this New Year's Eve was going to be different because I couldn't stay the whole night. I'd told Becky I'd pick her up at her house at nine to go to Michelle Edelton's party. I was not only sad, but I was anxious, too. I hadn't gotten around to telling Spencer. I didn't want to deal with him being disappointed or giving me a lecture, but because I put it off, it was now going to be that much worse.

The pizza came around 6:45, and we started playing and eating at the same time. By 8:00, I already had two houses on *Wicked* and a hotel on *A Chorus Line,* and he owned Idina Menzel, Ethel Merman, and Bernadette Peters. (He changed the railroads to Broadway divas.) Even though we have fun, we actually take playing very seriously because whoever loses has to buy the winner lunch on the first day back at school. That was another thing I hadn't brought up. How can we do the buying-lunch thing when we don't even sit together at lunch anymore?

By 8:15, I knew I had to tell Spencer that I couldn't spend the night. Which, of course, meant lying.

Spencer rolled a five and landed on *Mamma Mia!* He took a minute and then decided to buy it. Oy. As long as he didn't decide to see it. That show is a headache.

He looked at me, and I knew this was my moment. I bent over and held my stomach.

"Ow!" I moaned, hoping my years of acting classes would pay off.

"What's wrong?" he asked.

"My stomach." I moaned. "I think that pizza was bad."

"Justin." Spencer put seventy-five dollars in the bank and looked at me. "Do you remember when you wanted to miss your cousin's wedding so you and I could see *The Simpsons* premiere on TV that night?"

"Yeah . . . ," I replied, doubled over. My cousin, who was

much older than me, had the nerve to schedule his wedding on the one Sunday in September I looked forward to all summer.

"How did you finally get out of going?"

I paused, then stopped doubling over and sat up. "By using the technique you taught me for faking a stomachache."

"What are you trying to get out of?" he asked. "Losing the game? You can still buy Audra McDonald and stop me from having a diva dynasty."

"That's not it . . . ," I started, then faded out.

"Then what is it?"

I quickly looked at my watch, and when I looked back up, I knew he knew.

"Justin," he said while putting his cash in piles, "let's just count our money and decide who won based on that." He looked at the wall clock. "Let's see, if you started your stomachache now, you probably have to be somewhere by . . . eight forty-five?"

"Nine o'clock," I clarified.

He just shook his head.

"Listen," I tried to explain, "of course I'd rather spend the night here like I always do. . . ."

"But . . . ?" he asked.

"But I have obligations now."

"Obligations?" Spencer said, using major hand quotes. "You don't have obligations—you have deceptions. You deceived Becky's father into thinking you're dating her; then you deceived Becky to stop her from auditioning for the show. . . ."

"That's not true—" I began.

"By omission," he clarified. "As well as deceiving Becky into thinking you're helping her by pretending to date her when you're actually just doing it because you're after Chuck. And, of course, deceiving Chuck by not telling him you like him."

"*That's* not true!" I said.

"What isn't?"

"I don't *like* Chuck. I love him!"

Spencer's eyes widened. "That's what you think love is? Thinking someone's good-looking?"

"It's not just that," I retorted. "He's good-looking *and* popular. Everyone likes him."

Now he was really mad. "That's not what love is! You don't love someone's attributes!" Spencer started counting on his fingers. "Love is enjoying spending time with someone, respecting each other's feelings, being comfortable to be oneself with each other. . . ."

Oneself? Who speaks like that? And why does Spencer have to make everything sound so boring? Who wants to make out with someone's feelings?

Spencer seemed to calm down. "Justin, I know you don't have to be at Becky's until nine." Then he took a deep breath and said, "But I think you should leave now."

I couldn't believe it. I'd canceled plans with Spencer before. Once, I told him I was going to an all-day Clean Up Our

National Parks outing and I bailed after a half hour of raking leaves and took the bus to the mall. Why was tonight such a big deal?

"Can't I be popular and still have you for a friend?"

"Justin, I know we'll always be friends."

Phew.

"But I don't think we can be friends right now."

Oh.

I left my Monopoly money in a pile and picked up the overnight bag I came with that didn't actually have any pajamas in it.

I put on my coat and scarf (no hat because I could deal with the flu but not with having my carefully arranged 'fro ruined before the party). I opened his front door and turned back around. He was standing by the Broadway Monopoly board. "Happy New Year, Spencer," I said.

"I hope it will be, Justin."

I walked out into the cold. I knew I could handle Spencer not being friends with me for the time being, but I decided that it *also* meant he didn't get to be in my head anymore. No more ruining my fun with his "Are you really sure this is the right thing?" and "Why don't you think this through?" echoing through my cranium. I stopped walking so I could use one of Spencer's annoying spiritual techniques against him. I "visualized" (as he loves to say) him walking around inside my head, spouting off his killjoy comments. I then appeared inside my own head and walked up to him. I took his arm and escorted him kindly to the side of my brain, which I visualized as a cliff overlooking a deep canyon. I then gently pushed him the hell off. Bye-bye, downer.

Feeling cleansed, I quickened my step. Becky's house was four blocks away, and I wanted to get there soon so I wouldn't freeze. When I turned onto Pearl Drive, I suddenly saw Mary Ann Cortale appear out of the snowy darkness. She was wearing what looked like a coat I had recently read about at Greenpeace.org. It was made from completely recycled tires and plastic. Unfortunately, it also looked like that's what it was made from. I assumed she was walking to some low-echelon New Year's party. I didn't know whether to wave or not. We never really had been friends, and now that I was with the popular kids, we were very separated. While I was wondering what to do, I saw a figure step directly behind her. Doug Gool! I couldn't believe he took his harassment off school grounds! I knew Mary Ann didn't realize he was behind her. Popular or not, I had to help her.

"Mary Ann! Look behind you!"

Mary Ann turned around and saw Doug, who looked in shock. Not at Mary Ann seeing him, but at me warning her. He suddenly bent down, picked up some snow, and dumped it onto Mary Ann's head. She just stood there and Doug ran away.

I rushed over to her. "Are you all right?" I asked.

"Yes, Justin. Uh . . . thanks."

She kept standing there. I had assumed she was going

somewhere but then I thought maybe she was coming from somewhere. That would be depressing. Returning home so long before midnight. I didn't want to ask and embarrass her, so I just muttered, "See ya," and kept walking toward Becky's house as Mary Ann stayed in the same spot. What a strange night.

I got to Becky's house early, but of course she was ready. And looking beautiful. She had on a green top and jeans that managed to look casual *and* dressy and that brought out the emerald green in her cat eyes. Her dad came downstairs and was obviously also getting ready to go to a party.

"Justin, my boy!" he bellowed. "How's my bio whiz?"

I smiled (with dead eyes). "Fine, sir. Thank you."

He turned toward Becky. "He's a keeper, Becky! This boy is polite *and* destined to be a doctor."

"I don't know, Dad," Becky said, obviously annoyed. "He could easily go into theater. He's really good, you know."

Her father laughed. "I know he is! I've seen him perform." Then he added, "And he always comes through. That's the mark of a true professional."

"Thank you, sir," I said, getting uncomfortable with the nonstop praise.

"It's a hard field, Justin, as I'm sure you know. I've seen all of Becky's performances, and I've always told her, 'If you want to make it, you have to be perfect.'"

Huh? "How can you perform perfectly?" I wanted to say. *Theater and music aren't the Olympics.*

I knew I shouldn't argue, so I just nodded a lot.

"Speaking of perfect," he went on as he started tying his tie, "I heard you aced the mouth and larynx bio quiz."

It creeped me out that he always knew stuff about me, but I understood that Becky had to keep him informed so he'd keep believing we were dating.

"Well," I said, trying to make a joke, "I've always had a soft spot for the soft palate."

He laughed so hard I thought he was going to cough up *his* soft palate. He pointed to me. "*And* he's funny!" He finally stopped laughing and said, "You kids have a great time." He gave Becky a quick kiss as he walked to the kitchen. "Becky, your mother and I are going to the Epsteins."

Becky started to get her coat. "OK, Daddy," she said stiffly. Even when she was in full shutdown mode around her father, she still had that Becky beauty glow.

We walked out of the house and started toward Michelle Edelton's place. Becky's family was pretty loaded, but Michelle's were R-I-C-H. Becky told me that Michelle's room was in a whole separate wing of the house, which meant she could have parties and her parents never knew. Becky and I were quiet until we left her driveway.

"Sorry my dad is such a loser," she said.

I shrugged. "It's part of the deal," I said.

She stopped walking. "Is this worth it to you?" she asked. "I mean, you do so much just so I can keep on seeing Chuck. What are you getting out of it?"

"Well," I began, trying to walk quickly because it was freezing, "I don't know if you know, but I wasn't exactly the most popular kid before I started 'dating' you."

"So," she said, nodding, "you're doing it to make more friends."

I nodded as well, opting out of adding "and to steal Chuck from you." PS, it's not like I want to split them up. I just want to also get to date him. And if that broke them up, it wouldn't matter much because Becky's so beautiful, she could date anyone she wanted. I then got excited because my thought process wasn't immediately followed by Spencer's voice in my head telling me that I'm just thinking of excuses for my selfishness. Yay! His stupid visualization technique actually worked!

As we were walking to Michelle's house, I thought that this party would be the perfect vehicle to really make friends with these people. I'd do some of my imitations and, hopefully, there'd be a piano so I could play and sing. I'm sure I could win the cool kids over with my humor/talent, and having them all in one room could make it happen.

We walked up to Michelle's house and Becky immediately pulled me toward the backyard.

"This is the best way to Michelle's part of the house," she said.

We passed by a bench covered in snow. Becky stopped for a moment. "That's where it happened," she said.

I felt my heart race because I knew she was referring to her first kiss. Then I suddenly had a thrilling thought: *Tonight could be the night I get* my *first kiss!* Even though I have no interest in alcohol, I'm sure some kids will have brought some. If Chuck is tipsy, I could get him somewhere isolated and let things progress. I'd read articles about guys in high school experimenting with other guys when they were "bombed." While I think alcohol is responsible for many of the problems in society today (drunk driving, bad karaoke, unintelligible tweets), it could pay off for me make-out-wise!

"Let's go!" I said to Becky, and pulled her toward the side door. It was unlocked and opened right into a staircase. We walked up and there was a crowd of about forty kids hanging around Michelle's bedroom, which was the size of my living and dining room. I did a quick scan and saw that not only was there no Chuck yet, but there was also no piano. Argh! There goes my plan for wowing people with my voice. Also, the "DJ" (Archie the baseball player) was blasting music, so I couldn't even do my signature imitations because nobody would hear them. Well, if I couldn't rise in popularity, I better get my kiss out of Chuck once he gets here. Becky and I started moving through the crowd. There were a lot of people I knew from Cool U, but there were also kids from private schools in the area.

Becky asked me if I wanted to dance, and I said, "Sure" and she replied, "What?" I responded by moving her to the area where people were dancing and we started in. Of course, I wore an outfit I thought was slimming, but it also happened to be a wool sweater. Within ten minutes, I was dripping with sweat. I went out onto Michelle's balcony to cool off for a while and then came back in to dance again. This went on for an hour or two, with breaks only for soda and the amazing food Michelle had laid out. Finally, around 11:30, I heard a loud "NO WAY!" and looked over to the corner to see Chuck and three of his buddies from the football team passing around a beer can. They must have just gotten there from another party, and they looked drunk. Excellent! I knew Becky would want to be over there with him, so I moved her across the room.

"Becky!" he yelled, and ran to hug her. She hugged him back in a "we're just friends" way, and I put my arm around her to keep up appearances. Chuck realized they were in public and went back to his friends and a new beer can. They started passing it around and after a few minutes, Becky said we should go outside. I thought she meant to the balcony where I had cooled off, but she pointed to the backyard. She whispered in my ear, "Get Chuck," and she left before me. I told Chuck I wanted to show him something and took him by the arm. He was easy to lead because he was pretty drunk by now. While walking by everyone, I secretly pretended he was my date and we were going for a moonlight stroll. I chose to ignore the fact that he burped every four steps we took and called me Jeremy.

We finally got outside and I saw Becky by the bench where she had had her first kiss with Chuck. I walked Chuck over and brushed off the snow, and he plopped down with a thud. I sat next to him to keep him upright.

Becky looked angry.

"This is it? This is our New Year's Eve?"

"What?" Chuck slurred.

There wasn't any music drowning out her words in the backyard; he said "what" because he was too drunk to understand more than a two-word sentence.

She looked at me. "I thought tonight would be romantic." She pointed to the bench where I was sitting and Chuck was slumping. "I thought Chuck and I would ring in the New Year in the same place we started our relationship. But, of course, he'd rather spend time with his teammates."

"What?" Chuck said again, but this time it came out "Whaza?"

Becky stood up straighter. "Justin, I'm going." I made a motion to stand, but she put out her hand to stop me. "I can walk myself home. I'd rather you make sure he"—she pointed with disgust—"doesn't publicly embarrass himself and get thrown off the team." Typical Becky. Even when angry, she was still caring.

"Happy New Year," she said, and walked off through the snow.

I looked at Chuck. I looked at the house. Everyone was inside partying. We were totally alone. AND he was drunk. He was sitting pretty close to me. I was able to think he was snuggling with me to keep me warm. I looked over at him. Was he asleep?

"Chuck?" I asked quietly.

"Becky?" he answered.

WHAT? He thought I was Becky. This could be the way for me to get my first kiss. He's too drunk to know who he's kissing but not too drunk to not look gorgeous. I turned toward him. I heard someone in the house yell, "One minute to midnight!"

I thought, *My first kiss. With the boy I've always wanted to kiss.*

How should I do it? Lean in and hope he'll lean in, too? Put my hand on the back of his head and gently guide it? I did an emergency Listerine strip and ChapStick application, then turned back to Chuck, whose eyes were half closed.

Then I heard: *Is this really what you want?*

WHAT?

Spencer was back??? How did he climb up that cliff?

You want to get your first kiss by pretending you're someone else?

Yes! This whole "winning over Chuck" thing is taking a lot longer than I thought it would, and I need to speed the process along.

Really? So you want to have the memory of your first kiss be from someone who had no control over his body?

So what? The body he has no control over is the body of a Greek god.

Uh-huh . . . Is the drool on his lip the drool of a Greek god?

Quite frankly, yes.

"Becky, it's cold," Chuck suddenly said, turning toward me. "C'mere . . ." He snuggled up to me.

AH! He was essentially asking for it. *This is it,* I thought. I'm going to kiss him and who cares that it's all based on a multitude of lies.

OK, be my guest.

Yes!

But just know that one day you'll have to tell me about it in person.

I heard what sounded like tires screeching to a stop in my head.

I turned my head away from Chuck.

I let out a long sigh and saw my Listerine breath come out of my mouth like a cloud.

Forget it, I thought. Maybe I'm not speaking with Spencer now, but someday I will be. The time's gonna come when I talk about this night, and I know I could never look him in the eye and tell him this story. What would he think of me?

I sat with Chuck in the freezing cold while he fell asleep.

I thought of Spencer in his house. I wondered if he was still up.

I looked at the lights coming from Michelle's room and heard the people upstairs start shouting, "Ten, nine, eight, seven, six, five, four, three, two, one . . . Happy New Year!"

Happy New Year.

EVER SINCE NEW YEAR'S EVE, the weeks have flown by. School during the day, rehearsal for *Rock and Roll High School* in the afternoon, and Chuck and Becky at night. Well, a little Chuck, mostly Becky. Eighty percent of the time I show up for a Chuck/Becky date and it winds up being Becky and me waiting a few hours for Chuck and then discovering he's not coming. It hasn't been bad, though, because we end up doing our homework together and gabbing. In a way, she's taken the place of Spencer.

I don't share *everything* with her like I did with him (i.e., she doesn't know I'm actually gay and in love with her boyfriend), but she knows most everything else. And I think I know more about her than anyone else does. Even Chuck. She's told me about all the fights she's had with her parents (mainly shopping, school, and her hairstyle—her mother is originally from the South and Becky does a great imitation of her saying, "Why don't you grow it long? Like a real young lady."). I also know why her mom's side of the family hates her dad's side of the family (her dad's mom got drunk and threw up at their wedding) and how she and Michelle Edelton are friends even though she'll never forgive Michelle for trying to kiss Chuck at his birthday party (not surprisingly, I've never told her about my near miss with Chuck's lips on New Year's Eve). We do tons of talking not only at Cool U or during our waiting-for-Chuck dates, but also, oddly enough, at choir rehearsals. Of course, it's more like whispering there. Spencer and I say hi to each other at the beginning and end of the classes we have together and in the hall, but that's about it.

A few weeks ago, early in January, I wrote him a note apologizing for not telling him in advance about my conflict on New Year's Eve and left it in his locker. He emailed me that he got the note and accepted my apology. I thought we'd go back to the way we were, but he's still less friendly to me than I am to Mary Ann Cortale. He's obviously waiting for something to happen that will lead back to us being best friends again, but I don't know what it's supposed to be. It's very weird not having him know every little thing that's going on with me and vice versa. Even though all the boys sit in the same area in choir, Spencer is a bass and I'm a tenor, so he's on the other side of the group.

Thankfully, I don't have to sit in choir and watch him ignore me. The tenors sit right behind the altos, and Becky worked out having her seat right in front of me. She spends half the rehearsal twisted around chitchatting with me. Once in a while, Miss Bagwell will bust her for not facing forward and then Becky will always say, "What? I dropped something." She'll then bend down and pick up one of the many things we've planted there in case she gets busted. Normally, we put a book or a hair tie there, but last week, I hid the pencil case Becky planted and replaced it with a condom I stole from health class. I was hoping Miss Bagwell would bust Becky and luckily she did! Becky gave the same excuse she always did and bent down to pick up what she "dropped," but when she saw what I planted there, she burst out laughing. Miss Bagwell angrily asked to see what she had dropped, so Becky had to think fast. She was still bent down and frantically looked for the nearest thing to show her, which unfortunately was a piece of gum that someone recently stuck underneath her seat. She pried it off, sat up, and said, "Just my gum, Miss B." Then, to make it fully realistic, she *put it in her mouth*!

Talk about commitment.

The hilarious thing is, we're not allowed to chew gum in choir, so she got kicked out of class anyway. AND had someone else's skanky gum in her mouth. We spent all of lunch laughing our heads off. She really is fun to hang out with and is super-nice. So much so that I've been feeling more and more guilty during *Rock and Roll High School* rehearsal about Becky not playing the cheerleader. And I've felt even worse for myself because I have to play opposite crybaby Pamela Austin. I thought she cried that first day because Mrs. Hall asked her to cut her hair. Turns out she just cries at *anything* Mrs. Hall says.

"Pamela, please make sure you read exactly what the script says."

Nonstop tears.

"Pamela, please keep your arms raised until the end of the song."

Weeping session.

"Pamela, exit stage right."

HALF-HOUR crying jag.

And, of course, because I play opposite her, I'm the one elected by the cast to go "talk to her." It's always me telling her to "take a deep breath" and "have some water" and saying "I'm sure she didn't mean to . . ." After twenty minutes of me pretending I'm Dr. Phil, Pamela will finally wipe her eyes, blow her nose, *sloooowly* brush her LONG hair, and adjust her keyboard belt or treble-clef hair tie, and then we go back to the auditorium. When we start rehearsing again, she's relaxed and focused, whereas I'm constantly forgetting my lines or lyrics because I'm so stressed from spending a half hour forcing myself to pretend I don't want to strangle her with her music-note scarf. It's not fair! I began to think I was being punished for not convincing Becky to audition. It's almost like Spencer has a direct line to God . . . or, to respect Spencer's ever-changing non-traditional religious views, "goddess."

After a few weeks of rehearsal, the guilt I felt about Becky not auditioning was too much for me to bear, and I felt like I had to do something to make it up to her. My project became the upcoming choir solo. We're doing a *Wicked* medley, and I knew she'd sound amazing on the song "Defying Gravity," so every day at lunch I've tried to convince her to audition. I've received a slew of *no way*s and *stop bothering me*s from her, so two weeks ago I changed tactics and convinced her to come over to my house by saying I wanted her to try some brownies I was making for the choir bake sale.

That afternoon, I put them in the oven right before she got there so their smell would fill the air as she walked in. I knew the aroma would put her in a trance and I was right. While she was salivating, I told her that I'd only give her one if she sang through the solo with me. I could tell she was torn, but I sat calmly at the piano and waited because I knew that no one could resist that smell. The next thing I knew, she was belting out the song. I made sure to hide the picture of us in our *Cats* costumes so nothing could bring her down after she sang. I then took the brownies out of the oven, but held them at arm's length and said she couldn't have one unless she agreed to audition. She was feeling so good about how she sounded—and was so inundated with the delicious chocolate scent—that she said yes . . . and then immediately ate two brownies. Three days later she auditioned and got it!

Of course, I then began to worry that I had made a mistake. Yes, she sounded great in rehearsal but what about the actual concert and her tendency to crash and burn? And by "burn" I mean "sing horribly." My anxiety lasted right up to the concert, which was last Friday. Here's what finally went down: Her parents were out of town all last week at a medical conference (her aunt was staying with her), which was a bummer because it meant they couldn't be there to hear her sing, but Chuck promised he'd definitely be in the front row. Well, more like I threatened him that if he didn't show up, I'd tell Becky the real reason he missed dinner with her last Friday was not because of a late-night practice but because he went out with Archie and the gang to T.G.I. Friday's.

Of course, part of my plan was for Chuck to hear my solo "Free Your Mind." I hoped it would trigger something to make *him* free his mind and give guys a try. And by "guys" I mean "me" and by "try" I mean at least first base. I've had no progress with him for weeks. He had that first burst of flirting with me, but ever since then, he's been just mildly friendly. I don't want to think he was only flirting with me to get some cash and to have me do his homework. Becky wouldn't date someone so unethical, would she? So many aspects of my plan are working (well, mainly the popularity part), but time is running out on the Chuck front. It's getting closer and closer to my birthday (April twenty-first) and I still haven't had my first kiss. If it doesn't happen, that means on April twenty-second I'll be sixteen and a spinster. I'm trying every angle I have to get Chuck to cross over.

As the day of the concert approached, I got more and more nervous that maybe I'd made a mistake and was just setting

Becky up for another public debacle. Yet, the closer we got to the big day, the more relaxed she seemed. She was the total opposite of how she usually was before a big performance. The other strange thing was that we got together a few times knowing Chuck wasn't going to be there. She'd call me to watch TV or get a coffee and we'd hang out for a few hours. Of course, I missed staring longingly at Chuck, but we'd have a great time without him, so it was worth it.

Finally, the big day arrived, which also happened to be the last day of February, which this year was the twenty-ninth. I hoped that because leap year only occurs every four years, this would be the one concert in four years where Becky finally sounded great.

Unfortunately, I was wrong.

When I saw her before we went onstage, she looked great and relaxed. Instead of the horrible choir robe we're all forced to wear, she convinced Miss Bagwell to let her wear a black dress that had the essence of the Wicked Witch of the West but also showed off her amazing gymnast bod. She painted her nails green, which contrasted great with her red-gold hair that she wore loose and wild. When she walked up to the mic to sing, I nervously watched her, but she had a totally confident air I'd never seen in her during a performance. I was filled with anxiety that it would all fall apart, but the next thing I knew, she started the solo sounding even better than she did at rehearsal. Yes! I inwardly smiled, which only lasted around fifteen seconds because I then noticed her eyes spot something in the audience and in a nanosecond, she started to sound like a combination of my mom's car on a really cold day and my dog the week she'd had an obstructed bowel. When Becky finished, she got halfhearted applause and had tears in her eyes. I was angry. Not at her, but at whatever inside her was messing her up. How could such a popular and beautiful girl undermine herself like that? She had everything I wanted: looks, popularity . . . *Chuck*! Even when I was at my most loser-ish in the school, I still was able to perform. I didn't get it. But I had to figure it out. I wanted to help her. But first I had to sing.

Right after *Wicked*, we got ready to do "Free Your Mind." I went to the mic. For this number, they shined a big spotlight on me, which was fabulous, but it also meant I couldn't see the audience. Thankfully, I knew where Chuck was sitting, so I performed the whole song to him. I sang up a storm and every time I sang "free your mind," I concentrated as hard as I could, visualizing Chuck freeing his.

The song finished, I took my bow, and the lights went back to normal. Well, it was a good thing I had visualized Chuck because that was the only way I was gonna see him—*he wasn't at the concert anymore!* Once the spotlight was off me, I could see his seat and it was EMPTY. What the—? He must have left right after Becky's solo. How dare he only want to hear his girlfriend sing and not the boy who's trying to manipulate him to do something totally against his nature? I put my wasted effort out of my mind and ran backstage after the concert. I found Becky looking pale and asked her not to talk to anyone. I then said I'd change out of my choir robe and told her to meet me at the Roasted Bean. She nodded silently and I went to the boys' changing room.

I got out of my robe and met up with my parents, who were waiting for me in the lobby.

"Son," said my dad as he hugged me. "I don't know if you're going to join my practice after all!" This is the comment he always makes after he sees me perform. It's nice that he's so supportive of my talent but annoying that he's not creative enough to come up with another line.

Then my mom hugged me. "You were, as usual, excellent." Then she paused. "Your friend Becky, though . . ."

There were other chorus kids and parents standing near us.

"You mean my *girlfriend*, Becky?" I asked. I could tell my mom never fully accepted the Becky ruse and I didn't need other people joining her.

"Yes, Justin," she said halfheartedly. Then she shook her head and added, "She started out sounding so good."

"I know!" I said. "And I need to talk to her. Can I go out for a little bit? Just to the Roasted Bean?"

"Of course, son," said my dad, and as I'd hoped, he handed me a twenty. Yes!

"Bye! Love you both!" I yelled, and hightailed it to the street. When I got to my favorite coffee joint, Becky was at the only table near the fireplace, which gave us a nice view and some privacy. She had already ordered us two lattes, which were sitting there, steaming.

"Justin, I—"

"Whatever you're going to say, don't. Let's just decide that right now we are going to figure out why this happens to you and stop it."

"I don't know why!" she sobbed. "It's like . . . like my body won't let me perform the way I want to perform."

"But *why*?" I asked, frustrated. Why would someone's body sabotage them? "You've got to figure it out. I know you have the talent to make it as a performer."

She shook her head. "I'll never know." Then she looked angry. "And I'll *never make it*," she cried, loud enough for an older couple to look over at us, even though their table was across the room. She lowered her voice, but it made her next sentences more intense. "*Don't* say I will. No one cares about rehearsal." She wiped a tear from her eye. "It's how you sound in performance that makes you a star. If you want to make it, you have to be perfect."

That's a crazy theory, I thought. Then . . . *Wait a minute, I've heard that before.* I tried to think of when. I remembered the feeling I'd had when it was said, that the person talking was a bully . . . and an idiot. Doug Gool?

Then it hit me!

I looked into her eyes. "Becky, do you know who you sound like?"

She seemed to stop caring. "Who?" she asked with no energy, and leaned forward for a sip of her latte. Hmph. Well, if she was going to break this dramatic moment, then I was also gonna get some delicious latte. I took a sip and dropped the bomb: "Your father."

"What?" She looked like she had just drunk a latte with sour milk. Well, she did use soy milk, which is a close second, but I knew it wasn't that. She hated to be compared to her father.

"That's exactly what your dad said on New Year's Eve. He must have told you his stupid theory so many times that you believe it."

She thought about it, then shrugged. "Well, so what if I believe it or not? I still sucked tonight like I always do whenever I sing in front of people."

I was annoyed. "You do *not* suck when you sing in front of people. It's not like you rehearse by yourself in an isolation chamber."

She rolled her eyes. "You know what I mean."

"Yes, but I think that's the key to figuring this out. You're able to sing in front of tons of people at rehearsal but not during a performance. And it's not like you can only sing in front of people you're used to," I reminded her. "We had a dress rehearsal for the choir concert on Thursday night with all the band and orchestra members in the audience and you nailed that solo." I added two more sugars to my latte and posed a question: "What was different about the audience at the choir performance versus the dress rehearsal?"

"Who cares?" she asked, frustrated. "I always mess up when it really counts."

I was about to say something when she cut me off with: "Listen, high school's only for a couple more years. Then I won't perform anymore." She sneered and said, "There's no singing and acting in medical school."

I grabbed her hands. "Medical school? You can't go there. You should be majoring in theater. You're amazing!"

She pulled away. "No, I'm not!" she said. "Besides, my dad would never allow me to go to a theater school because he knows how bad I am when I perform."

I suddenly got an idea. "Well, tell him you were perfect tonight. Tell him you've changed. He'll never know!"

"Of course he will, Justin," she said, putting down her mug. "He was there."

I was confused. "What? Your aunt's been staying with you because your parents were at a convention all week."

She nodded. "Yeah, but he left it a little early to come hear me."

I had a feeling this was important. "When did you find out that he flew back here, Becky?"

"Well, after the concert he waited for me and told me that instead of flying back tomorrow morning, he had switched his flight to today so he could see me." She looked frustrated. "Why do you want the details? We both know my dad is annoying."

"Wait," I said, not letting her change the subject. "You mean, you didn't know he was there until after the show?"

She sighed, obviously bored with the conversation. "Before

the show, I thought he wasn't coming, but a little after I began singing, I saw him in the third row."

AHA! I knew she had seen something in the audience after she began singing. I just didn't know what it was or how it related. Now I knew why she sounded great at the beginning of her solo and then clanked. I grabbed her hands tightly, and she looked at me like I was crazy.

"That's it! The missing link! Don't you see?"

"That you're weird? Yes, I do."

"No, you fool!" I said, and leaned in toward her. "You sound great in rehearsal because your father isn't there judging you. But every public performance you give, he's sitting there and you know what he's thinking." I imitated his stupid, pompous voice: *"If Becky isn't perfect, it will prove yet again she can never be a performer."* I went on. "No wonder you panic and bomb. Who could handle that pressure?"

She thought about it. "He does come to all my performances. . . ."

"Exactly! And because you know he's there waiting for you to mess up, you do!"

She looked thoughtful. "So, what do I have to do? Ban him from ever seeing me perform?"

I shook my head. "I'm not sure. But now at least we know what it's about. Once you know something, you can deal with it!" And with that, I took an enormous gulp of my latte and finished it, leaving only a trace of sugar granules on the bottom of the mug. I felt great relief. And saw that Becky finally looked like her old, stunning self again. I looked at my watch.

"We better go, Becky!" I said. "Especially if you want to get in one of your good-night phone calls with Chuck."

She waved me away. "Oh, we don't do that anymore." Then she sighed. "I think we've become like those couples who are used to each other and gradually fade out."

What? Could it be? The field could soon be open for me to snag Chuck? I don't want to make them break up, but if it happens, it sure is good for me!

Becky put down a tip. "Let's walk home the lake way," she said.

There's a quick route to get home or there's a longer, more scenic one that goes around the lake.

"OK," I said, and we headed out.

On the way home, I thought Becky was nervous we'd run into some kids from school, because she held my hand. She was smart. I hardly thought anymore about proving I was her boyfriend, but it was better to be safe than sorry.

By the time we started walking through the park, I assumed she'd want to speed-walk because it was cold, but when we got to Goose Pond she motioned for me to sit with her in the gazebo.

"Thanks, Justin," she said, looking at the water. "For helping me."

"Well, it's semi-selfish on my part," I said. "I love good singers and I want you to become famous so I can obsessively listen to your CDs on my iPod."

"You know," she said, moving closer because it was so cold, "I appreciate all you've done and your friendship, and I was thinking . . . maybe there's more to it."

More to what? More to my theory about her dad?

She continued. "Chuck is so wrapped up in football it's like he doesn't know I exist. He didn't even stay after the concert. But you . . ." She smiled.

I was dazzled. I knew she could be a star. To have so much talent and be that beautiful was rare.

"You're a real friend, Justin. And lately I've been thinking we should continue where this is leading."

Again with the double talk, I thought. *Where* what *is leading? Why so much mystery?*

She stared at me. I didn't know what I was supposed to say. I was just cold.

"My point is, if you're interested, I'm interested."

She leaned even farther in. And it wasn't because it was cold. I suddenly realized it was for something else and I didn't know how to stop it.

No!!!!

Unfortunately, yes.

Well, the goods news is, I won't be a sixteen-year-old spinster.

I've had my first kiss.

12

SO MUCH HAS HAPPENED IN the last few weeks. And not happened. My popularity, which I was sure was going to skyrocket, is actually at a standstill. And, weirdly enough, the only difference between September and the spring is I've gone from having at least a *few* friends to having *none*! Yes, now I'm *friendly* with everybody at school, but I don't feel I have any actual *friends.* At least when the year began, I had Spencer as a best friend and our little group at lunch as my other friends. I mean, it wasn't like I called any of them to hang out (besides Spencer), but I always liked it when they'd confide stuff in me or ask my advice.

This afternoon, I was really needing a dose of connecting with someone who's known me for a long time and was thankful to see Quincy Slatton ahead of me on the line for the salad bar. *Ah!* I thought. *Someone from the old lunch gang!* He's the science genius who's only a sophomore but is already taking physics. When we used to eat lunch together, he'd always ask my advice about dealing with his younger brother, who he shares a super-small bedroom with.

"Hey, Quincy! How's your brother?" I said with a big smile as I took a huge ladleful of honey-mustard dressing.

Quincy got a confused look and glanced over his shoulder, as in, *Is there a popular kid named Quincy you're talking to?* He then looked at me like he was asking permission to speak.

Silence.

I didn't know what to do, so I finally nodded as if giving him permission and he quickly said, "Um . . . it's fine. He's fine." He then looked away and tried to put some cherry tomatoes on his salad but missed his plate and dumped them all onto his tray.

That's it? He used to talk to me nonstop about whether he should make a line across their bedroom delineating who had what side or if he should get a permanent marker to label all of his stuff.

"I'm sure he's fine," I said, wanting to actually have a conversation. "I was wondering if he's still using your stuff."

"HAHAHAHAHAHA!" Quincy laughed as if I'd made the funniest joke in the world. What was the joke?

"Quincy?" I said, cutting him off kindly. "I wasn't trying to be funny," I clarified.

Silence.

"I'm really asking you," I continued.

"Oh," he said, "uh . . . my stuff's fine." He then gave a crazy smile and had to swallow several times.

Why couldn't Quincy act normal with me? He sounded like I did when I talk to my aunt Rhonda, who I only see every two years when we go to New Jersey for the High Holy Days. Or how I sounded last year when a senior from Cool U talked to me when we were both on a bus with our moms because it would have looked weird to them if we ignored each other.

I figured Quincy was stressed from some horrible AP science exam and waited for him to launch into a story about his brother wearing his sweatshirt or breaking his gene-therapy experiment.

Silence.

"OK, Justin," he said as he hurried away, "thanks for talking with me."

What the—?

I stayed at the salad bar and saw him sit down at our old lunch table. Pamela Austin was there with him and two freshmen I didn't know. I felt jealous that they got to eat with Spencer. Oh yeah, he still hasn't really spoken to me. After New Year's, I was so busy, I didn't even notice him gone from my life, but now I wish I could talk to him again. I miss how I used to be able to tell him anything, and how we used to make each other laugh all the time. Yes, I make the kids at Cool U laugh, but nobody makes *me* laugh. And no one ever makes plans with me or shares anything real about themselves. If I happen to be alone with any of them, I try to find common interests, but they always just want to gossip about the other kids. I need to get as close to the Cool U kids as I was with Spencer. I'd hoped that all of them would come see me in *Rock and Roll High School* last month and be so blown away by my big number that they'd finally want to be real friends. But, even though I'm part of their gang, seeing a musical was still too uncool for them, and only Becky showed up.

Which brings me to the problem I never thought I'd have—breaking up with somebody I'm not really even dating in the first place! Ever since Becky gave me that first kiss, I've had to play an exhausting game of never being alone with her. I wish I could tell her that even though she's beautiful with a great personality, I'm just not interested in girls . . . but I've only had the courage to tell Spencer I'm gay, and that was by accident. Instead, I told her *and* Chuck that my rehearsals were getting too intense and I couldn't meet with them until after show weekend.

I thought Becky would cool off after a few weeks and forget she was ever interested in me, but instead she keeps emailing me and asking when we can hang out again without Chuck. I simply don't reply, and if she brings it up during school, I either feign that my spam filter is acting up or shake my head and say, "You didn't get my email? I totally wrote back!" and then flee without telling her what I supposedly wrote back.

The problem is, once *Rock and Roll High School* ended, I was supposed to go back to meeting with them so they could have their dates, but I couldn't risk showing up and having Chuck be massively late as usual because that would leave me alone with the mad kisser. I had to come up with another plan, so I've started hiding out in front of wherever we're all supposed to meet and I arrive only *after* I see Chuck. I get a lot of studying done as I'm waiting, but it's hard to do a take-home test or write an English essay while crouching behind a bush. My system is I give Chuck an hour, and if he doesn't appear, I text Becky and say I'm tied up practicing violin or piano or that my mom is forcing me to clean my room/the garage/the yard. She'll then text back, asking for some private time, and I write her back with nonsense words that look like my iPhone autocorrected them:

> We can get together tumeric. What tumor don't yodel
> want? I can only meet Freedom and showered night. See
> you therefore!

I'm exhausted from the multitude of lies I have to keep juggling. This whole "pretending to date Becky" has reached new levels of complicatedness, and it has to end.

Last week I mentally decided that I'd keep it up until the Spring Fling, which, by the way, happens to be tonight. Yes, having Becky as a "girlfriend" made me more popular, but I'm hoping everything's going to change 100 percent at the dance tonight, because Mrs. Hall is in charge of the entertainment this year, and I've convinced her to let me perform!

Since it's a dance, the school DJ, "JJ Gangsta" (aka Josh Epstein), is going to spin. However, a few weeks ago, I went to Mrs. Hall's office and told her that when the Spring King and May Queen are crowned, it would be great if there was a live song to go along with it. The king and queen always take a slow walk through the crowd on a red carpet, and every year it's accompanied by the DJ playing whatever song of the day is popular that has some kind of message about love or special-ness. I know Mrs. Hall is always frustrated that the musicals don't sell out, so I told her it would be a great advertisement for the theater department if we did a live song from *Rock and Roll High School*. She thought about it and then asked what song. I said, innocently, that there were two that could work: "The Best Night" (which is about a girl who's having the best night of her life) or "Our Love Will Last" (which was my big number). Pamela sang "The Best Night" and I knew Mrs. Hall wanted nothing to do with that crybaby again, so the next thing I knew, she was asking me if I'd sing my song!

Finally. I'll get a chance to show all of Cool U my talent, which will hopefully make my popularity reach the level I've always wanted it to. And that will lead me to Chuck.

Oh yeah, that's the big news! Ever since the chorus concert, I'd pretty much given up on Chuck. I shook off my denial and realized that there are some guys, even if they're totally straight, who will use their good looks with anyone to get what they want. His "flirting" with me was just his way to get some easy cash out of me and have his homework done. Yes, I would still gaze at him in class, but I accepted that my first kiss wouldn't be from him. And yet, I was still enjoying the little bit of closeness I felt to him by doing his French work. Every day, we'd follow the same system of him surreptitiously putting his French homework into my book bag while I walked in front of him out of class. Thankfully I hadn't put a stop to that because it led to something that could change everything!

One week ago, I was sitting under one of the trees near the parking lot. I went to take out the French quiz Chuck had slipped into my bag that morning, and I decided to dump my whole bag onto the lawn because I hadn't cleaned it in months. I'm notorious for using my book bag as a repository for anything I don't know where to put in my room. Well, lying on the ground, amidst the old Roasted Bean receipts and notes I've passed in class for the past few months, was a brand-new book I'd never seen before. Since no one else has access to my book bag, I figured Chuck must have slipped it in that morning, but I didn't know why. I looked at the cover, which had a picture of a really cute high school baseball player. Oh no. Was this Chuck's thank-you for me doing his homework? A boring book about sports? Typical. I know he's pretty self-centered and he probably thinks that every kid loves sports as much as he does. The title of the book was *When I Figured It Out*. Figured *what* out?? Sports were a snoozefest? I don't need a book to tell me that. I looked on the inside cover to see if he wrote anything to me. Nothing. When I turned it over to look at the back cover, I saw another picture of the same cute baseball player from the front cover . . . but this time his arm was around another boy. And it wasn't a "we're just buddies" pose. It was a "we just made out" pose. What the—?

I suddenly became interested and started flipping through the book, and turns out it was filled with essays about kids who were typical straight boys in high school. You know, "playas" with steady girlfriends or a different one every week. But every single one of them . . . was gay! They were just too scared to be who they were. Why would Chuck put that kind of book into my bag? I guess he could have done it because he thinks I'm gay and he was trying to be caring. But *caring* isn't a word I associate so much with Chuck. He's not mean or anything; he just seems to look out mainly for his own interests.

Then it hit me.

Chuck must have put it into my bag for one reason: to tell me that underneath his typical straight exterior was a gay kid who needed my help coming out!

AH!

It was all I could do to stop myself from running to his locker, screaming, "I'm a-comin', Chuck!" and giving him my grandmother's engagement ring she promised I could give to my fiancée one day.

But then I thought there must be a reason he left me a book and didn't just come right out and tell me. I decided I should read the book. And by "read" I mean "scan." I looked at the first story, which was about a jock like Chuck (ice hockey, though, not football). He had a girlfriend all through high school even though he'd known he was gay from the time he was twelve. He wrote that he couldn't admit it to anyone because he was so scared of disappointing his parents. Is that what Chuck's going through? I've never met his folks, but they're probably typical sports parents and want Chuck to be the All-American straight kid.

Hmm. I couldn't really identify. With my parents, it's almost as if they *want* me to be gay. They keep politely asking about Becky, but I can tell they're hoping we're not together anymore.

I continued reading (see previous definition of "read"). Most of the stories had the same themes. The fear of parents turning against them or the fear of losing all of their friends.

I thought about the friends part. I realized that one of the reasons Chuck wouldn't date me is because I'm not on his popularity level. If he dated me while I was at my current status, he'd definitely lose half his friends. That's when I realized how perfect my plan is to make everything work out tonight. If my song brings down the house (which I know it will), my popularity could rise to heights I've never achieved before. I would be almost at Chuck's level. If I had *that* kind of school-wide acceptance, I wouldn't be scared of coming out to everybody (including Becky). And my newfound status would then open the door to me and Chuck dating! I wouldn't be able to do anything about his parents approving of him or not, but my soaring popularity would hopefully make Chuck realize he could date me and still be the king of Cool U!

And, yes, I know the relationship will not last a long time. Even if Chuck is 100 percent gay, it doesn't change the fact that we don't have much in common. I just want to know what it feels like to kiss him and then have the most popular kid in school as my boyfriend. Even for a few days.

So, the good news is I may finally get to kiss Chuck, but the bad news is, it won't be my first kiss like I'd always planned. I can't stop thinking about that night Becky told me it's something you never forget. Great. I'll "never forget" the image of trying to avoid those unwanted, incoming lips mixed with the feeling of my butt freezing. It's so unfair that Becky has the romantic images in the garden with Chuck and I have depressing flashbacks to the horrible night in the gazebo. It's not really her fault, though. I made her think I had already had my first kiss. She didn't know she was forever ruining something I'd always fantasized would be perfect. Speaking of perfect, I have to get my outfit ready for the dance. So much is riding on this night, I can't afford for anything to go wrong!

13

HMM . . . IT'S HARD TO KNOW what went wrong first.

I'll start from the beginning. I got home from school, did my homework, had dinner, and then started a long vocal warm-up. I had only one chance to impress the whole school and I didn't want to blow it because I had a phlegm attack. I sang through my song twice, took a long shower, and then put on my Spring Fling outfit—dark jeans, new black cowboy-type boots, and a gray and black button-down shirt from H&M. I wore the shirt out in an "I'm so cool I don't have to tuck in my shirt" kind of way, even though it was really in an "If I tuck my shirt in, you'll see my stomach flab hanging over my pants" kind of way. I may have lost weight in the last few months but not enough to dare tucking anything in.

I went over my lyrics as I walked to Becky's house and finished the song right when I walked up her driveway.

Her father answered the door and ushered me in.

"Becky!" he called upstairs. "Your prince awaits you." Then he laughed so hard he had a small coughing fit.

Becky arrived at the top of the stairs in a dress that was tight in the right places but didn't make her look like she was trying to show anything off. She wore a green necklace that made her eyes even more stunning.

She came downstairs and gave me a little smile. "Hello, Justin . . . *finally.*"

"Finally?" said her dad, looking at his watch. "He's actually early."

Becky glared at him because he ruined her moment. She was obviously trying to bust me for avoiding her. I was happy he distracted her and took the opportunity to ask if we should go.

"I'll drive you," said her dad, putting on his coat.

Yay, I thought, *Becky won't be able to confront me while her dad is in the front seat.*

"I have to go anyway," he continued as he got his car keys. "I'm a dance chaperone."

My *yay* turned into *noooooooooo!!!!!* I had no idea her dad was going to be lurking in the gym all night. It sucked because that meant Becky really couldn't spend any time with Chuck . . . meaning she'd be with me the whole time . . . meaning I'd have to endure nonstop barbed comments or, worse, another smooching session.

Becky and I drove there in silence while her father

chattered about medicine and, for some reason, the pituitary gland. He knew we were studying the endocrine system in biology and kept talking about how "the pituitary gland is overlooked by the majority of the medical establishment." It's also overlooked by anybody wanting to have an interesting conversation!

When we walked into the school, Quincy was sitting at the door of the gym. I hadn't seen him since our awkward non-conversation at the salad bar. He had a camera and I realized that he was in charge of taking photos of all the couples entering.

"Hi, Quincy!" I said as Becky and I walked up.

He went pale immediately and dropped his camera.

Becky and I stood there while he picked it up and put the batteries back in.

"Uh . . . ," he said, not making eye contact, "you can stand there." He pointed to a backdrop that was supposed to look like a garden. Since it was the Spring Fling, everything was spring-related. Quincy nervously positioned Becky so she faced away from me. Huh? Was she supposed to look like she was ignoring me? I stood awkwardly until she angrily grabbed my arms and put them around her waist. Oh! It was that kind of pose. I had never come to the Spring Fling with a date, so it was all new to me.

"Becky, why don't you smile?" asked her dad, who unfortunately hadn't started his chaperoning duties yet.

Quincy started counting, "One, two . . ." as her dad traced

upward lines next to his lips to indicate to Becky that she should smile. I think she ignored him because as soon as the picture was taken, her father muttered to Quincy, "Hopefully the camera broke when you dropped it."

Becky and I walked in with her father, and I chose to believe she wanted to keep up the same pose we had in the picture and that's why she was still completely turned away from me.

The inside of the gym was a spring paradise. Savannah was on the design committee and the place looked gorgeous. She had commandeered the art class into making fake flowers out of some material that looked real and they were *everywhere.* Covering the floor and the stage, hanging from vines, and blanketing every tablecloth.

"Well, I have to go monitor the punch," said Becky's dad. "I don't want any kids having hangovers tomorrow." He laughed and was met with silence from us. "Uh . . . have fun," he said, then added, "Or at least talk to each other." As Becky's dad walked away, she started walking in the opposite direction.

"Becky!" I called after her. When I got near, I whispered, "Are you going to look for Chuck?"

"Why should you care?" she said without looking at me.

"I just meant you should be careful because your dad's here."

"My dad?" she asked. "Don't worry, Justin. I know how to

handle *jerks*!" She made the first eye contact of the night when she said "jerks."

As she walked away, I began to feel guilty for how I'd treated her since that kiss at the pond. Argh! How was I supposed to win over Cool U with my amazing performance *and* snag Chuck if a part of me was wracked with guilt?

I was feeling so stressed that I knew I needed some potato chips to deal with my anxiety. I turned to walk over to the food area and suddenly saw Spencer. He was holding hands with someone. I looked closer.

It was a girl!

What the—? I thought he was gay. Well, I was, too, and *I* was here with a girl, but that's different. I looked closer but couldn't tell who the girl was. She had long hair and a pretty face. But there were little marks on the sides of her nose from where glasses probably sat. And the dress looked like it was made of organic cotton. Wait a minute . . .

It was *Mary Ann Cortale*!

I knew she'd look good with no glasses and her hair down, but was she really here with Spencer as a date? I had decided they were just here as friends when I saw him give her a quick kiss on the lips before she walked toward the drinks. I stood frozen, which put me in line with Spencer's eyes. He walked over to me.

"Hey, Justin."

"Spencer," I said slowly, "are you here with Mary Ann?"

"Yes," he answered simply.

"On a *date*?" I asked, in total shock.

He sighed. "It's complicated," he said, which was an even more bizarre answer than I'd expected.

"Spencer," I said, lowering my voice, "you told me you were gay. Are you now experimenting with—"

"Shhh!" he said, and looked around. "I don't want to have this talk now, but there *is* something else we need to discuss."

Phew, I thought. *He finally wants to start being friends again.* Being so close to him made me really feel how much I missed him. I wanted to tell him everything that'd been happening—Pamela's crying jags, Becky's unwanted kiss, Chuck and his possible coming out—but mostly I just wanted to hang out with him. I couldn't wait to pick up where we left off.

"Yes?" I asked, waiting for his apology for ignoring me, which I would accept graciously.

Instead he asked, "Are you happy?"

I was confused. "At the dance?" I asked. "Not really. I wanted potato chips but when I saw you and Mary Ann—"

"No, Justin," he said, cutting me off. "Are you happy in general?"

It was such an odd and non-specific question. Was he offering support? Advice? I thought about it. Happy? I was excited about the chance to perform tonight. And I was hopeful it could win me some real friends *and* my first kiss from Chuck. But I wouldn't say I was happy. And, thinking about it, I realized that I hadn't been for a while. More like stressed, guilty, lonely, and anxious.

"No," I simply answered.

"Well," he said with a little smile, "I'm glad you didn't lie."

"Why would I lie?" I asked.

Then I remembered.

NO!!!!

The public dare! I told Spencer months ago (to get him off my back) that my whole popularity plan would make me happy and if it didn't, he could make me do a public dare at the Spring Fling! I had assumed that whole bet was nullified when we stopped talking, but apparently Spencer didn't.

"Justin," he said solemnly, "you made a promise and I know you're going to keep it."

He was right. The public dare was sacred. I knew if I didn't follow through with it now, we could never have another one when we became friends again.

I took a deep breath. "What is it?" I asked.

He spoke slowly and clearly, like he had practiced it. "You need to start being yourself in front of people."

THAT was the public dare? Act like myself? I do that already. Pretty much. Except for the things I keep a total secret.

Uh-oh.

"What do you mean?" I asked.

"You've been telling me forever that you're in love with Chuck."

"Yeah . . . ?" I asked nervously.

I did say that, didn't I. Hmm. I don't know now if *love* is exactly the word anymore. More like *lust*. But I can't admit that to Spencer because he'd been saying that all along. Suddenly, he revealed what I had to do.

"Your dare is to admit it tonight."

Hmm . . . that sounded pleasingly vague. "What do you mean by 'admit it,' Spencer?" I wanted to hear what Spencer had to say so I could spin the dare to my advantage.

Spencer could tell what I was doing and got annoyed. "Justin, you need to admit—"

At that moment, we both noticed creepy Doug Gool slowly walking by, obviously looking for someone to harass. Spencer clammed up because he knew that if Doug overheard, it would ruin the public dare of me admitting anything since Doug would tell everyone first. Spencer started talking in code. "Justin, you need to admit to the *person* you're in love with that you're in love with *them*."

Hmm. I guess I could tell Chuck I was in love with him and then later tell him I was joking.

Of course, Spencer was on to me, so he made it a dare I couldn't manipulate. "You're not allowed to say something and then take it back."

Hmm . . . well, maybe I could—

"And you can't say it like you'd say it to a friend."

Argh! Why can he still read my mind?

Doug Gool was still lurking, so Spencer kept up the code.

"Justin, you need to give 'them' a kiss."

Thankfully, Doug Gool slowly started walking away. He was probably looking for his favorite target: Mary Ann. Maybe Spencer was there as her protector. If he was, he wasn't doing a very good job. Regardless, I had to figure out how to deal with this public dare.

"Tonight?" I asked, even though I knew that's what he wanted.

"Yes, Justin." Then he added the obvious: "In front of the school."

Well, my plan *was* to win Chuck over tonight. I had assumed we'd meet up after the dance, he'd tell me how impressed he was with my performance, and we'd end up smooching. I guess I could make it happen quicker. Right after I perform, I could pull Chuck onstage and just go for it.

Unless . . . what if my song works even better than I thought and Chuck can't control himself? *That* would be an amazing way to bust Spencer. Here he is, trying to bust me in front of the school, but what if the joke's on him?

"Spencer," I asked slowly, "what if *he* kisses *me* first? Does that count?"

It was one of the only times I've seen Spencer at a loss for words.

"Uh . . ." He thought about it. "I guess so."

Then he paused again before adding, "Good luck, Justin."

And with that, he walked away toward the "bar."

And suddenly I was face to face with Becky.

The impossibility of the dare suddenly hit me. I was supposed to kiss her boyfriend in front of her? Even I wasn't willing to do that. It's one thing to do it behind her back, but I didn't want to publicly humiliate her. I'd have to renege on doing a public dare for the first time in the history of my friendship with Spencer. But before I told Spencer to forget it, I knew I had to clear the air.

"Becky," I said, "I need to talk to you."

"Really?" she asked angrily. "After not talking to me for weeks?"

I nodded. "Yes. I'm sorry."

"Sorry? Is that what you say after you could barely stand to touch me when we had our photo taken outside the dance?"

"What? No." Now she thought everything was a rejection from me. "It wasn't that I could barely stand to touch you. I didn't know what I was supposed to do."

"Oh, come off it, Justin," she said. "You're just a tease. You get me to like you and then when I finally do, you act like I'm disgusting." And with that, she ran out of the gym. I went after her (first stopping to finally get a handful of chips) and caught up with her in the parking lot.

She was sitting on her father's car. "Becky, I don't think you're disgusting," I said while still chewing. And panting. "I think you're beautiful."

She looked at me like I was crazy. "You think I'm beautiful? Then why did you cut me off after that night at the pond? We used to have fun hanging out . . . and then nothing." She started crying. "Why would you hurt me like that?"

"Becky . . . ," I began, and then stopped. I could make up some lie about having a cold sore and not wanting to spread it, or I could tell her the truth.

You should tell her the truth.

Good ol' Spencer. Just as intrusive as ever.

I took a deep breath. How was she going to take this? Would we be friends past this next minute?

"Becky," I began again, "don't you think Rachel Deena is beautiful?" Rachel graduated last year but was hardly around all senior year because she got "discovered" in a mall and after that was always flying to some far-off country to do a modeling shoot.

"Yes, I think she's beautiful," she said, annoyed. "Why? Are you dating *her*?"

"No," I said. "My point is, just 'cause you think she's beautiful, do you want to kiss her?"

"Of course I don't," she said, as if I were a moron.

"Exactly," I said.

"Justin," she said, frustrated, "you're not making sense. I wouldn't want to kiss her because I wouldn't want to kiss any girl. I like boys."

I was silent.

She gave me a look like *And????*

I stayed silent.

Then an expression came on her face and I knew she knew.

"Ohhhh . . . ," she finally said. I raised my eyebrows. "But . . . ," she began, "but . . ."

"But what?" I asked nervously. Was she about to tell me she didn't ever want to speak to me again?

"Why didn't you tell me?" She wasn't crying anymore, but she somehow looked more hurt. "I thought we were close."

Why didn't I tell her? "Well, I was scared," I admitted. I realized I was the same as a lot of kids in that book. "I didn't want you not to like me."

"I could *never* not like you," she said warmly. "Even when I hated you, I still liked you."

It made no sense, but I knew what she meant.

She got off the car to give me a hug, and when she did, I felt a big weight lift off my shoulders.

"So, you've never told anyone?" she asked.

"Only one other person," I explained. "My friend Spencer." Then I added, "Who's not really my friend anymore . . ."

"Hmph," she snorted, "like Chuck's not my boyfriend anymore."

WHAT?!?!

"Becky! For . . . for real?" I sputtered.

She nodded.

"Since when?"

She got back onto her dad's car. "Since around a week ago. I began thinking about breaking up last month. Right after the concert when you helped me realize my dad was ruining my performances."

I certainly remembered that night. It ended with the infamous kiss.

"I began to realize who I wanted to be with."

"Me?" I asked nervously.

"Well"—she smiled—"yes. Or at least, someone like you. Who listens to me and worries about me and tries to help me."

I nodded. She went on. "Chuck is a lot like my father—he cares mostly about himself and what he wants. He's a terrible boyfriend."

I nodded again, but inside I thought that maybe he sucked as a boyfriend because he didn't really want a girlfriend.

"So, if you broke up with Chuck, why did we have to go to the dance tonight?" I asked. "You don't need to cover up for your father anymore."

She looked at me like I didn't get anything. "Justin. I wanted a chance to spend time with you. The past few weeks you've been avoiding me nonstop." She laughed. "I guess you were afraid I was going to attack you again."

"Well, it wasn't really an attack," I said as I got up onto the car with her.

"Oh, please, it was exactly like my first kiss," she said with an eye roll.

Huh?

"Your first kiss?" I asked, confused. "I thought that happened in Michelle's garden and it was perfect."

"Oh, it was," she confirmed. "I'm talking about my *literal* first kiss, not what I consider my first kiss," she explained, making me more confused.

She must have seen my expression because she launched into an explanation. "Justin, everybody knows that you can get kissed a lot of times before having your first kiss."

"Meaning?" I was hoping something would finally make sense.

"Meaning," she said, as if I were a little slow, "your *first kiss* is the one where you feel fireworks. The one where you think you're in love, or you could be in love. The one or ones you get before that don't count. Your actual first kiss is the one you'll always remember."

Ohhhh!!!

I smiled because I think I got it. And because there was hope for me.

She went on. "When I was in summer camp, I had to team up with one of the guys in the other bunk during Color War. When we won the rowing competition, he leaned across the boat and kissed me." She shuddered with the memory. "I was totally not into him, but I couldn't escape him in that tiny boat."

Hmm. Sounds like a certain bench in a gazebo I've experienced.

She went on. "It was technically my first kiss but it doesn't count. I got kissed a few more times since then, but it wasn't until Chuck that I felt I *really* had my first kiss."

Wow.

So that means I'm still waiting for mine.

And, hopefully, Chuck's going to give it to me tonight!

14

WELL, SO FAR A FEW things had gone wrong at the dance, but I felt like I was managing them all. After our talk, Becky and I left the parking lot and headed back to the gym. It was weird to be with her and have her know everything. Well, not everything. She still didn't know that I'd been trying all year to get Chuck to date me. I thought I'd save *that* reveal for a more appropriate time. Like in a letter from college. Hopefully, when Chuck and I smooch tonight, Becky'll think it was one of those spontaneous, crazy things and not because I'd been scheming since fall. I walked back into the dance and saw that the big glass jar near the punch bowl was getting filled up with the ballots for the Spring King and May Queen.

Then I noticed Mary Ann getting punch. Spencer, her supposed date/protector, was nowhere to be seen, but horrible Doug Gool was lurking. Ever since New Year's, I've been swooping in and saving her from him. Maybe it's been my way of staying close to Spencer. I know I upset him when I didn't sit with them the day Gool put chocolate on her pants, and I guess I've felt like I've been making up for it with my vigilantism. Sometimes I'd see her waiting in front of the school and Gool'd be turning the corner, so I'd run up, frantically tell her to follow me, and bring her back into the school and out the side exit. Once, I was at the mall (the day I was shopping for my Spring Fling outfit) and I saw Mary Ann sitting depressingly by herself at the food court. Then I caught sight of Doug in line at the Rockin' Wok. It's one thing to be harassed at school, but I think it's doubly embarrassing to have it happen in public. I did a preemptive strike by grabbing her hand and running with her to the elevators.

I was happy that I could look out for her. No one ever helped me when I was Doug's biggest target, and I would have loved someone like me getting me out of his way. I noticed that Mary Ann's dress was completely white (dye would probably ruin the organicness of it), and I could just imagine Doug "accidentally" spilling some red punch all over it. I didn't want her to always carry around a horrible memory of this dance, so I made a beeline over to her.

"Come with me!" I said forcefully, and put my arm around her.

"But—" she started.

"You'll thank me later," I said as we hurried away. I saw

Spencer by the food, deposited Mary Ann next to him, took another handful of chips (all right, two), and went to the boys' room to start prepping (aka flossing) for my performance.

Right when I was gargling, in walked Becky's dad. I braced myself for another boring conversation. Hopefully he was sick of the pituitary gland and would move on to the lymph nodes.

"Well, well, well," he began, "fancy meeting you here!" He laughed at his own unfunniness, which led into his signature coughing fit.

I smiled politely and maneuvered past him to leave. I was thankful to see him go toward the urinal as I was walking out, but then he had the nerve to continue the conversation! I was at the door when he said, "Justin . . ."

I slowly turned around and soon heard the unmistakable sound of liquid flowing. "Yes?" I said uncomfortably.

"What are your plans for the summer?" he asked while continuing at the urinal. It seemed like forever. How much did he drink before he entered?

"Um, I'm going to go back to Usdan. It's an arts camp." I turned to go again. "See ya."

"That's too bad," he continued, talking *and* peeing. "I thought maybe you could join Becky at the hospital."

Hospital? Is she sick?

"What's the matter?" I asked nervously as I turned back around.

"Oh, nothing's the matter. Quite the opposite." *Finally* he started to zip up. "I got Becky an internship in the endocrinology research laboratory starting in July."

Oh. So that's why he wouldn't stop talking about the pituitary gland. It was obviously on his mind. Wait a minute. I didn't remember Becky telling me anything about it. During chorus rehearsals last month, I told her how great Usdan was, and she told me she was thinking of going to the May auditions.

"When did she apply?" I asked. It must have been during the weeks I was avoiding her.

"Oh," he said as he flushed. "She didn't apply. I called Dr. Markowitz, who runs the unit, and told him a little about her and he agreed to take her as an intern."

What a depressing way to spend your summer.

"Is it a morning or afternoon internship?" I asked. Maybe she could do Usdan for a half day.

"Both," he said matter-of-factly. "Every day from eight to six."

It sounded awful.

"How do you know Becky wants to go?"

He had the nerve to look at me like I was bizarre . . . after having just had a full conversation with me while peeing!

"Justin," he said as he walked to the sink, "it doesn't matter if she wants to go. Her mother and I decide what's right and wrong for her."

Was this the 1800s? "Sir," I said, which I only say when I'm really angry at an adult and trying to feign being respectful, "Becky doesn't want to go into medicine. She wants to be a performer."

He put his arm around me (thankfully, after washing his hands) and said, "Have you heard Becky in performance?"

I knew he was going to bring that up. "Yes, I have, but more importantly I've heard her in rehearsal and she's got an incredible amount of talent."

"That may be true, Justin, but I'll tell you something that's obvious to anyone with eyes and ears. She doesn't have any confidence. And *that's* what you need to make it."

And with that he walked out.

How dare he? He's the one who set her up for failure by saying she had to be perfect to make it. And because of that pressure, Becky always failed. Turned out, he'd known all along she didn't need perfection. That must have been his way of undermining her confidence so she'd follow the path he'd chosen for her. What a sneak! I had to tell her.

I ran out of the bathroom just in time to see Chuck about to enter the party . . . with Michelle Edelton! Wow. He went from one fake girlfriend to another, just like those guys in the book he got me.

"Yo! Justin!" Chuck called from down the hall.

I walked over quickly. "Hey, Chuck. Hey, Michelle," I said as I sized her up. Hmm, she was my competition in one sense, but I knew the real Chuck underneath. He wanted boys.

"Are you here with Becky?" he asked me, and Michelle laughed.

What was the funny part?

"Yeah . . . ," I said warily. I was feeling protective of her.

"Well, I'm sure she told you that we don't need you for a cover any longer," he said, putting his arm around Michelle.

Boy, he was pushing the "I like girls" shtick with me. Did he not know I read (skimmed) the book he gave me?

"Yes, Becky said you guys broke up."

"Were you surprised?" he asked, and his eyes glimmered.

I wanted to say, "Not really because I know you're gay," but I didn't want to push it before my performance. I needed him to know that the cool kids accepted me before I made my move. I decided to go another route.

"Well, I noticed you weren't too upset when you started to miss dates because you had to be with the team."

Both he and Michelle let out a little laugh. I didn't like the sound of it. Then she whispered flirtatiously, "I didn't know you called me the team."

He nudged her jokingly and said, "Be quiet, you!" then gave her a quick kiss.

WHAT? Did I just hear that right?

He was dating Michelle at the same time he was dating Becky!

"See ya, Justin," he said, and they walked into the dance.

I didn't get it. If he was secretly gay, why was he cheating on Becky with Michelle? Did he really have that deep of a need

181

to prove to everybody that he was a lady-killer? And did people still use the phrase *lady-killer*? (I'd heard it in an old Lauren Bacall film on TCM.)

It's one thing to be in the closet and feel the need to cover up by dating a girl, but it's another thing to *cheat* on that girl, especially with her close friend! Why hurt someone just to perpetuate your own image?

What a creep. It was getting very hard for me to fully support my plan to win him over. If we did start dating, what would stop him from cheating on me with one of *my* friends?

GASP!

Like Spencer! If Chuck went behind my back with him, I'd have a breakdown.

I then forced myself *not* to think of myself (for five minutes) and thought about poor Becky. Her father was horrible *and* her so-called (closeted) boyfriend had been cheating on her for who knew how long. As I was thinking about her, I happened to look up and caught a glimpse of Chuck from the back.

Holy cow!

He must do a lot of squats. And did his shoulders get broader? I pondered whether he was born with that V-shape or if it was from all the pull-ups he did in the weight room.

OK, focus! This new development meant I had to ponder the situation objectively; I accept that Chuck will never be a long-term boyfriend and that he could cheat on me the same way he cheated on Becky, but quite frankly, even if we date for a month, I'll have memories to last me for the rest of my life. And think what it would be like in college if I showed prospective boyfriends photos of Chuck and called him my ex. I'd be able to date the hottest guys in school with that kind of pedigree.

Suddenly, I heard Spencer's voice in my head.

Stop your plan now, Justin. How do you think Becky will feel if you kiss Chuck in front of her?

Um . . . slightly mortified?

Take out the word slightly.

OK. So, you're saying I should just do my big number, get the whole school to finally worship me, have more friends than I've ever had before—

People who worship you aren't your friends.

But—

No singing. No Chuck.

But I have to follow through with the public dare, don't I?

You know I'm only making you do that so you'll accept who you are.

But what about my personal responsibility toward my school? There's a music performance scheduled for the crowning ceremony. I don't want to let down Mrs. Hall.

Really? Or do you not want to give up getting attention?

What'd you say? The connection's going in and out. Are you in a tunnel?

Nice try, Justin. I'm in your head. Listen to my advice.

ARGH! I wanted to discount his babbling, but whether in

my head or in real life, Spencer's been my voice of reason, the one who's not afraid to tell me things I don't want to hear. And he always does it in a caring way. A caring, annoying, know-it-all, spoil-the-fun way.

Spencer's voice was strong, but so was the one telling me that I worked so hard to get to this night—scheming with Becky, winning over Cool U, dealing with Becky's dad, getting close enough to Chuck to have him secretly admit his biggest secret, trying to *not* get too close to Becky, convincing Mrs. Hall to let me sing. How can I give it all up when I'm almost at the point of getting what I've always wanted? School-wide adulation and a first kiss from the hottest guy I've ever known!

Because it's wrong. You don't love Chuck.

But it'll feel so nice to kiss him.

Will it feel nice to hurt Becky?

SHUT UP!

OK. That's it. I needed to get rid of Spencer in my head and *I* needed to decide what's right for me.

Spencer!

Yes?

Clear out. I need time alone.

I think you need—

Don't make me push you over that cliff again. I'll do it.

Fine. I'm outta here.

Spencer?

Spencer?

Silence.

OK.

Thinking.

Thinking.

Then it hit me.

The solution.

Yes! I probably knew it all along.

But I had to figure everything else out as well.

Hmm . . . hmm . . .

I stood in that hallway for ten minutes with a dazed look on my face. But I wasn't dazed; I was P^2: planning and plotting.

Got it!

I went into the dance and saw that the big glass bowl by the punch was empty, so all the forms for the Spring King and May Queen were backstage being counted. I had to move fast. I found Becky chatting with Savannah and company and gently pulled her away.

"What's up, Justin?" she asked while I maneuvered her over to a private corner.

"Becky," I said intently, "I hate to say this, but . . . did you know that Chuck was coming with Michelle?"

She looked surprised for a second and then sighed. "I guess so." Then she clarified. "I mean, he didn't tell me. But I've been hearing the gossip about it in school." She then added, "I told you he was a jerk."

I refrained from commenting.

OK, now on to the second bomb-dropping.

"Listen . . . ," I said, trying to ease into the bad news and then just deciding to plunge in. "Your dad is planning on sending you to intern at a hospital this summer."

"What?" she asked, confused. "I told you I want to go to Usdan. I still mean it."

"I know, I know," I said, and then recounted the whole horrible bathroom conversation to her.

"Oh, Justin," she said, sounding overwhelmed, "what am I supposed to do?" Then she looked away, into the distance. "It's always going to be like this, isn't it?"

"No! It doesn't have to be," I said with conviction. "But first"—I turned her around and looked her in the eye—"I need you to do something."

"Now?" she asked.

"Well, soon," I explained. "When they crown the king and queen, I'm going to play the piano and sing a song onstage."

"You're going to sing?" She gave me a quick hug. "That's amazing!"

"Will you turn my pages?" I asked, and before she could answer, I pulled her to the stage.

At that moment, Principal Berman began testing the microphone. "Hello, students!" he said with the smile he turns on only when parents are around. "It's time for the big event of the evening. The crowning of this year's reigning couple."

Everyone started cheering, and Becky and I made our way to the piano onstage.

"Justin," she said in a panic, "where's the music?!"

"Don't worry," I said as we sat on the piano bench.

Mr. Berman ripped open a gold-colored envelope. "Please welcome your new Spring King and May Queen . . . Chuck Jansen and Michelle Edelton!"

I wasn't surprised. That was the power of Chuck. Even though he just started dating Michelle (in public anyway) a week ago, they were already being crowned king and queen. Everyone started cheering wildly. I looked out into the audience and could see Spencer standing at the foot of the stage, looking at me and shaking his head slightly. I smiled and waved to him. I knew that after Chuck and Michelle got crowned, Mr. Berman would read the boring list of "Royal Duties" they were to assume, so I had to seize my quick window of time.

I gazed at Chuck, who was approaching the stage with a giddy Michelle. The light was hitting his face just right, making his already white teeth glimmer. I shook myself out of my stupor and ran up to the front of the stage with the microphone from my piano. "Congratulations, King and Queen!" I yelled, and everybody cheered again. Then I added, sounding incredibly positive, "Who cares if they deserve it? They're the *winners!*" Everybody cheered again, obviously not taking in the content of my sentence, just the tone. I saw Spencer raise an eyebrow, and I knew he got my passive-aggressiveness.

"While the king and queen take their triumphant walk," I continued, "we're going to part with tradition tonight and have a hot, *live* performance instead." Thankfully, I still got cheers. Spencer went back to shaking his head. "So, listen up, everyone!" I yelled, all the way to the back row of people. "Right after the rules are read, get ready for . . . Becky Phillips!"

Everybody cheered and I ran back to the piano as Mr. Berman started reading the traditional rules list. "King and Queen," he said in an uncomfortable monotone, "you are to spread joy like spring flowers, blooming throughout the year. . . ."

When I got to the piano, I saw that Becky's face looked like mine last year when I realized the camera was filming me in the locker room. "Justin, what are you doing?" she hissed.

I smiled and moved her off the bench. "You're going to sing 'The Best Night,' the song you should have sung in the show."

"Wh-what?" she sputtered. "I don't know it!"

"You told me you'd memorized every song in the show."

"I don't want to sing." She folded her arms defiantly. "I'm not doing it!"

"Becky," I said calmly, "don't pretend you don't love performing. Here's a chance to do it in front of the whole school."

I could hear Principal Berman droning on: ". . . must present themselves in a respectful manner . . ."

"But . . . but . . . ," Becky sputtered. "Chuck's here with *Michelle*." Then she somehow got even paler. "And worse than that, my *father* is out there." She was almost sobbing. "You know what that does to me."

I spoke soothingly. "Becky, c'mon. We'll deal with it."

My calming tone must have gotten through to her. She got color back in her face and didn't say anything for a minute. Then she looked like she was getting an idea. She started scanning the crowd. "OK, this *could* work if you think you can convince my dad to leave." She started fumbling for her phone. "You could call him on his cell and pretend to be—"

"No, Becky," I said, cutting her off. "When I say 'deal with it,' I mean deal with the fact that he's here."

She looked panicked again. "No, Justin! You know I can't perform with my dad in the audience."

"You're going to have to, Becky, because there'll *always* be someone out there like your father. Someone who'll doubt you or try to sabotage you." I could tell she didn't quite know what I meant, so I explained. "It could be another singer who's trying to bring you down or one of those mean and stupid critics. . . ." It looked like I was making her even more nervous, so I grabbed her by the shoulders. "But *none of them* can take away your talent." I locked eyes with her. "The only thing they can take away is the joy you feel when you sing." Then I said as strongly as I could, "Don't let them!"

I could tell she was torn. She kept looking at the stage, then at the audience, then back at me.

I channeled my inner Spencer to come up with the perfect line.

"Becky, do this performance and you'll be free."

I saw something register in her eyes, and right at that moment Principal Berman ended his litany of boringness. I handed Becky the microphone and she slowly started walking to the center of the stage.

She looked nervous and turned toward me for help.

I looked at her and simply said, "Hospital internship."

She got an angry look on her face and yelled, "A-one, two, three, four!" and I launched into the intro to the song.

Chuck and Michelle started taking their red-carpet walk but no one looked at them. Everyone was watching Becky, who had never sounded better. I was so happy for her. Halfway through, her father moved all the way to the front of the stage. I didn't know whether he wanted to see her performance up close to prove to himself it was really her or if he was trying to psyche her out. It didn't matter. Becky belted out the final chorus, and when she got to the last note, she leaned down and sang it right to her father. People in the audience probably thought she was giving him a shout-out, but I knew it was more like the finger.

When she finally cut off, everyone started cheering wildly. Chuck and Michelle stood in the back, on the red carpet, waving like the applause was for them. When Chuck waved, I could see the bicep in his arm go up and down. Ahh. He and Michelle started making their way back to the stage as Becky ran over to me and gave me an enormous hug.

"I did it, Justin! I did it! I didn't crack once!"

"Or go flat and sharp at the same time!" I added, but thankfully the crowd's cheering was too loud for her to hear my unnecessary specification.

I pushed her back center stage and told her to take another bow. She bowed twice and ran offstage smiling and laughing.

Chuck and Michelle had made their way back to the stage, and I decided to go through with the public dare. I couldn't break tradition. And I knew Spencer had to be onstage for it, so I walked to the microphone.

"Everyone, listen up," I said. "I'd like to congratulate our king and queen." There was applause again but not as much as there had been for Becky. "And because I have a duty to fulfill, I'd like to call Spencer Larsen to the stage."

There was a smattering of applause, which quickly faded out. Spencer looked at Mary Ann and then at me. There was silence while he decided what to do. Everyone was looking at him, and I knew he wouldn't be able to take the public awkwardness. Sure enough, he started walking onstage.

I was standing center stage, with Chuck right next to me and Michelle next to him. Even though Chuck and I were in the same light, for some reason it made *his* skin give off a glow. Ahh. Once Spencer came onstage, I tore my eyes away from Chuck and started talking to the crowd again.

"I've been given a challenge to show who I am tonight."

I started to get nervous but also excited. Becky had said that your first kiss was the one you had with the person you loved or could fall in love with.

"I'd just like to tell everyone out there that, no matter where you fall on the cool meter, you deserve friends. And you deserve people to be nice to you." I tried hard to express what I had come to realize while standing in my trance in the hall. "Unfortunately, though, you will one day have to face the fact that not everyone is going to like you, or like your friends, or your boyfriend or girlfriend."

"What's your point, Goldblatt?" yelled Vito Klimzak, one of Doug Gool's sidekicks.

Oddly, I heard nothing from Gool himself. Ms. Horvath (E.R.) shushed Vito, but that one sound must have strained her voice because I saw her immediately clutch her hand to her throat (under her neck brace) to soothe it.

I tore my eyes away from her and said, "My point is, it's time to show this school who I really am."

Dare I say it all?

Yes.

"And more importantly"—I decided to use good grammar as a shout-out to Ms. Horvath—"*whom* I really love!"

I saw Ms. Horvath approve of my grammar with a nod. Not surprisingly, that seemed to send her neck into another spasm.

"Go for it!" someone shouted from the back.

I looked at the whole audience—Quincy, Savannah, Mary Ann (with Doug, of course, lurking nearby). I saw Becky standing near the front of the stage with her dad. She had a perfect view. I then looked at Chuck and his blue eyes and his dimple and his sparkling ivory teeth. I savored his looks and then said a silent *goodbye* in my head. I took a deep breath, popped an emergency Listerine strip into my mouth, and in front of the whole school, I had my official first kiss.

With Spencer.

HOW DO I WRAP THIS up? I guess by telling everything that's happened since the dance. Hmm ... I'd better first finish telling what happened *at* the dance.

When I went to kiss Spencer, most of the audience definitely went into shock but none more so than Spencer. I had kept my eyes open as I approached his face, and not only was I almost blinded by his bright red hair (which, of course, looked amazing) but I also saw his eyes open wider than I've ever seen them. It was like those close-ups they have of actors in disaster movies when they see the White House being blown up or the Golden Gate Bridge being eaten by a monster. But as soon as I locked lips with him, he closed his eyes and I closed mine. Mmm ... I'm happy to report that it was exactly as Becky told me it would be. I remember it as a perfect combination of hot and cold: fireworks *and* chills.

Spencer and I broke away, and almost immediately the

shocked silence of the crowd turned into lots of applause and cheers. *And* lots of boos. With a healthy dose of "fags" thrown in. I didn't even look to see who was doing which. It finally made no difference to me if the kids from Cool U approved or not. My whole dream of the school worshiping me was officially over. It ended when I was standing in that hall being harassed by Inner Spencer and I took time to calmly think. At that moment, an enormous fog was lifted off me. I realized how crazy it was to ever think I would get the whole school to want to be friends with me. And even if I could do it, they wouldn't be friends with *me;* they'd be friends with a version of me I'd have to work nonstop to maintain. It felt so good to realize I could just be myself and have real friends like Becky. After I figured that out, I suddenly realized who I really wanted to kiss. Yes, Chuck was gorgeous, but once I found out he was fooling around with Michelle while he was with Becky, I got the opposite of a "talent crush," hereby known as a "personality repulser." I could look at Chuck and appreciate his stunningness, but I knew I would feel grossed out to actually kiss him. Yes, I had sympathy for him if he really was in the closet, but that didn't give him an excuse for cheating on Becky. Or being self-centered. Or flirting with me just to get something. Or never paying me back my twenty dollars!

After all my fantasies of Chuck were cleared out of my head, they were replaced by thoughts of Spencer. He was so sweet and supportive of me, and I always thought he was cute. I just never really took more than one second to think about how much I liked him because my mind was so preoccupied with Chuck or my stupid popularity plan.

Back to what happened after the kiss: Spencer and I separated and I stuck out my hand.

"Friends?" I asked.

He stuck out his hand but didn't shake mine yet.

"Boyfriends?" he asked tentatively.

"Yes!" I yelled, then shook his hand and had my *second* kiss.

And with that, I looked at Mrs. Hall near the sound booth, pointed to her, and said, "Back to the music!"

The DJ started blasting a Beyoncé song that made Ms. Horvath hysterically clutch her neck brace with both hands, implying that the volume of the music could somehow make her head fall off. I rolled my eyes at Spencer as we walked off the stage holding hands. Then I realized my mistake.

"Sorry about that," I said quickly.

"About what?" asked Spencer as we made our way across the dance floor to a quiet spot down the hall.

"Well," I began, waiting for the sermon, "I . . . uh . . . sort of rolled my eyes at you when E.R."—I quickly corrected myself—"I mean, Ms. Horvath acted like . . ."

"Acted like Beyoncé's volume was going to make her head separate from her body?" he finished for me.

"Yes," I said sheepishly.

"So why are you apologizing?"

"Because I know"—I tried to remember how Spencer would put it—"that eye rolling is poison for the soul . . . or bad karma . . . or something." I looked at him, hoping I'd said the right thing.

"Oh, Justin, stop," he said, looking at me with a grin. "I know I made you crazy this year with my spiritual-this and spiritual-that stuff."

I didn't know whether to admit it. "Sort of . . . ," I said, and trailed off.

"I'm sorry," he said. "That was a mistake."

"Um . . . it was?" I asked, trying not to show how hopeful I was that he'd dropped all of that.

He explained. "After that whole thing happened with Mr. D . . ." He stopped for a second. Mr. D was that teacher Spencer really liked who left the school.

He continued quickly. "I guess I was so upset that I thought if I immersed myself in some kind of spiritual quest, it would be cleansing."

I must have looked confused, because he added, "It was sort of like those body cleanses where you only drink juice for a month."

Ah. I nodded because I'd just read about those juice fasts in an article revealing how celebrities stay thin.

"Did it help?" I asked.

"I guess I do feel much better now. But it also prevented me from asking you out."

"You mean . . . you had thought about it before?" I asked.

He looked at me like I was a moron. "Justin, I've wanted to kiss you since my Labor Day barbeque."

HE DID? That was so many months ago! "Then . . . then why didn't you?"

He looked away. "Because I was an idiot. I thought that denying myself things I wanted would be good for me. You know, like a monk."

Who tries to be like a monk when they're fifteen?

"That's also why I went kosher," he added.

Wow. He found the most annoying parts of *all* religions.

I began to feel frustrated. If he had asked me out months ago, none of this stress would have happened. "Spence, if after a while you realized it wasn't really working, why didn't you stop your stupid self-denial and tell me you liked me?"

"I was going to," he said, annoyed.

"When?" I asked, just as annoyed.

"New Year's Eve."

Oh.

I smiled sheepishly. "I guess I messed that up."

He nodded. "We both did. I should have said something. But I was feeling jealous of Chuck."

"Then why did you want me to kiss him tonight?"

"I just wanted you to be happy." Typical Spencer. "If it wasn't going to be with me, I wanted you to stop torturing yourself about Chuck and just go for it."

"But what if somehow it had worked out?" I asked in a slight panic. "You know, if I somehow got to date Chuck for a while. I never would have known you liked me."

He smiled. "I went all those months without speaking to

you, Justin. I knew I could endure however long you dated Chuck."

"You would have waited for me?"

He nodded. "I would have waited for you."

I relaxed.

Then—

"So . . . ," I said nervously, "I also need to ask . . . have you stopped immersing yourself in all that Eastern religion/ meditation/kosher stuff?"

"Yes," he said, "for the most part."

I brightened up. "So I can go back to making fun of people?"

"No!" Spencer said immediately. Then he added, "Not unless they deserve it."

Yes!

E.R., get ready to be dished daily.

Uh-oh. I suddenly remembered: What about Mary Ann Cortale? Why did he have to start dating her on the night I kissed him?! Hmm . . . I guess I could demand that he break up with her, or we could sneak around behind her back until summer break. . . .

No. I couldn't do it. I had to speak up.

"What about Mary Ann?" I asked pointedly.

"What about her?" he asked, confused.

I grabbed his hand and walked him back to the dance floor. I didn't see her but knew we had to find her. "Before we do another thing, you need to tell her this is serious."

"Why?" he asked, sounding even more confused.

I was now getting extremely annoyed. "Because I'm not the kind of boyfriend who will let you have a girlfriend!"

Then he started laughing.

Rude!

"She's not my girlfriend," he said.

I was not amused. "Then why are you her date tonight?" I asked haughtily.

He suddenly stopped laughing. "Uh . . . I can't tell you that."

"What?!" I asked, furious.

"I'm sorry, Justin. But I can't tell you."

Suddenly I heard a horribly familiar voice.

"Yes, you can."

What the—? On the best night of my life, I had to still deal with him?

That's right, lurking as usual was Doug Gool. I guess he thought since I wasn't cool anymore, he could start bothering me again. Well, I suddenly realized, now that I'm not afraid of people knowing I'm gay, I'm also not afraid of him.

"Shove it, Gool!" I said, and gave him the finger. I started walking away with Spencer but then realized Spencer wasn't with me. He was still standing with Gool.

"You don't have to protect me, Spencer," I said as I waved him over. "Just walk away from him."

"Justin, come over here," Spencer said calmly.

Oh no. Was he back to his "we're all one under a loving spiritual being" business? I thought he gave that up when he started missing bacon.

"Justin," said Spencer. "I came with Mary Ann for protection."

"I know!" I said, frustrated. "And you didn't do a good job! Doug was right near her at the punch."

"I know, I saw," he said, laughing.

WHAT'S HAPPENING?

I then realized that I didn't *think* that last comment—I screamed it.

"Justin, calm down. I wasn't protecting Mary Ann from Doug. I'm trying to protect Doug *and* Mary Ann."

"From *what*?" I asked, at the end of my rope.

"He was protecting my image," Doug said. Then he looked at Spencer. "But you don't have to anymore."

Spencer looked confused. "Why not?" he asked.

"Because of Justin."

This conversation wasn't making any sense, but then Gool continued.

"Listen, Justin, " he said, looking me in the eye, "seeing you on that stage was inspiring."

Was this Doug's twin? I hoped not because two Dougs would make me want to transfer.

He went on. "You didn't care who knew you were a fag—I mean, who knew you were gay. It made me realize that . . ."

Doug trailed off but then suddenly stood up tall (aka to his full five feet five inches) and said, "*I* don't care anymore either."

Spencer actually hugged him, but I thought, *Oh no! Doug is gay? I don't want to belong to the same club he does.*

"Well?" said Spencer, waiting for him to do something.

"Justin," said Doug nervously, "I'd like you to meet someone."

"OK . . . ," I said slowly.

"My girlfriend," he said triumphantly, and presented me with . . . Mary Ann Cortale.

"But . . . but . . . ," I stammered. "Since when?"

Mary Ann actually spoke. "Since that day Douglas put chocolate on me."

That was the longest sentence I'd ever heard from her. Then I heard more!

"He called me that night to apologize."

Hmph. He never called *me* to apologize.

"And . . . ," she said shyly, "we wound up talking for a long time."

"I asked her out!" he said with a big, toothy grin.

It made no sense. "But you were always writing stuff on her locker!"

"That was so my gang wouldn't know what was up." Then he clarified, "Mary Ann's not really considered cool by my peeps."

But the word peeps *still is?* I thought. "But you were always about to attack her. I was constantly saving her."

"No, Justin," Mary Ann said, shaking her head. "We'd be out on a date and you'd see us near each other." She smiled at Doug, then at me. "The next thing I knew, you'd swoop in and end the date."

Spencer then spoke up. "Mary Ann told me what was up and I agreed to help them when I could. So tonight I was Mary Ann's 'date' so no one would know she was here with Doug."

"But I don't care anymore," said Doug. And with that, he dipped her and planted one right on her mouth.

That was a sight I never thought I'd see. Nor ever *wanted* to see.

He raised her from the dip and kept his arm around her. "Thanks, Justin," he said.

"And . . . ," prompted Spencer.

"Oh . . ." He hung his head. "And . . . sorry I was such a dick."

I was in such a state of shock that I let Spencer lead me away. We ran right into Becky.

"Justin!!!!" she screamed, and pulled me into a hug. "Thank you so much for tonight. Guess what? I'm not doing the internship!"

"Your dad canceled it?" I asked.

"I don't care!" she said. "I told him I'm not doing it no matter what and I'd pay for my own college if he wouldn't let me major in theater." She hugged me again. "I'm not scared anymore!"

Then she looked at Spencer and me. "And congratulations, boys!"

Spencer shrugged and I looked away, embarrassed. It was like when your aunt pinches your cheek and yells in front of your family, "He's so CUTE!"

Coincidentally, Becky followed her congratulations with, "Justin, he's so CUTE!"

I was still embarrassed . . . but happy.

"Can we all hang out together?" she asked hopefully.

"Well," I asked nervously, "would you ever consider sitting at another table during lunch?"

She smiled her stunning smile. "Yes! Let Chuck and Michelle sit with all of the other kids. I'd much rather sit with you guys!" We then did a group hug, and Spencer said he'd walk out with me.

We happened to take the long way home and passed by the infamous pond. I decided to have a new memory to replace the old. I brought Spencer to the little gazebo and planted one on him. Yes! My third kiss of the night and still as exciting as my first! We walked to the edge of my block and separated. I could see his orange hair almost all the way to his house.

I got home a little bit before eleven p.m.

Naturally, my mom was awake. But she wasn't working on the computer as usual; she was waiting up for me. I saw her in the living room, sitting on the couch.

"Your father got called to the hospital. But he said I could have this conversation without him."

Huh?

"Justin," she said while patting the seat next to her. "We need to talk."

Oh no. I hate when people say that to me. It always involves something I don't want to hear, something I'm being busted for, or some private, personal thing about them I'm incredibly embarrassed to hear about.

I slowly sat down.

"Yes . . . ?" I asked.

"How was the dance with Becky?" she asked stiffly.

"Uh . . . we broke up."

She perked up. "Really?" she asked.

"Yes. It's over." Then I added, "But we're gonna be good friends."

She smiled broadly. "Oh, I have no doubt about that. Most straight girls love to—"

Her hands shot to her mouth.

The unspoken rest of the sentence hung in the room.

No one broke the silence.

This was ridiculous. I had to tell her. Besides, the whole school now knew!

"Mom," I said loudly, "I'm gay."

She looked incredibly relieved.

"Oh, honey. I know." She hugged me tightly. "A mother always knows." Then she smoothed out her nightgown. "That's what I wanted to talk to you about."

"What do you mean?"

She suddenly started talking very fast. She was obviously thrilled to get this off her chest. "Becky's such a sweet, bright girl. Normally, she's so chipper, but I was shopping at the mall twice this month and both times I saw her eating by herself at Sushi Yummy." She shook her head. "She seemed so down."

I thought of Becky and felt sad for what she went through for those weeks. She had broken up with Chuck *and* I was avoiding her.

My mom kept talking. "I once dated a guy in high school who later turned out to be gay, and I thought maybe she was having the same feelings I had back then. The self-doubt, the constant worrying about being pretty enough." She took a deep breath. "Anyway, since the initial plan your father and I came up with didn't work, I stayed up tonight to ask you to break up with her. I hated to see her hurting."

It was sweet of my mom to be so concerned for Becky, but it was also annoyingly typical of her butting into everyone else's life. Hmm . . . maybe I'll suggest she take more than two courses a semester. She needs something else to do with her free time.

Then I thought . . . wait a minute.

Initial plan?????

"Mom . . . what plan of yours didn't work?"

"Well, we wanted to try to help you accept who you are. . . ."

Oy. She sounded like Spencer.

"So"—she shrugged—"we got you that book."

"What book?"

"What book?" she repeated. "The one I slipped into your backpack before you left for school a few weeks ago. *When I Figured It Out.* Did you read it?"

WHAT?!?!

She's the one who bought the book, *not* Chuck? But because of that book, I spent hours feeling sorry for Chuck. *And* it had helped me decide to kiss him at the dance.

I thought back to the day I found it. I had been about to accept that I'd never have him, but then the book gave me hope to follow through with my elaborate "Spring Fling" plan.

I looked at my mom. Yet again, one of her and my dad's crazy plans completely backfired. I was about to tell her how much trouble they both caused me, but then I thought, *What if I hadn't planned on kissing Chuck at the dance? Would everything have worked out this perfectly?* Maybe without the book, I never would have wound up with Spencer. It's like a house of cards. If you took away one card, maybe everything would have crumbled.

I smiled and gave her another hug.

"Thanks for the book, Mom," I said. "It really helped."

"Oh, honey, you're welcome." Then her eyes widened. "And, by the way, there's an online dating site for teens! Your father and I were talking about uploading your profile—"

Oy. Welcome to the rest of my life.

I cut her off and said I was super-tired and had to go to bed.

I'd tell her about Spencer tomorrow. Let her enjoy scheming with my dad tonight.

I got into my pj's quickly. It was the first night I fell asleep right away instead of lying under my quilt, planning the next day's deception.

The rest of the school year has gone by so fast.

I see Spencer almost every day after school either at my house or his. His mother is so liberal that she barely raised an eyebrow when he told her about us.

For my birthday, Spencer took me back to Nice Matin, where we had eaten brunch on the day we saw that Lincoln Center show months ago. I noticed a big wrapped present in Spencer's New York Civil Liberties Union messenger bag, and while we shared a chocolate mousse for dessert, he finally presented it to me.

I unwrapped the beautiful paper and . . . it was the Broadway-themed Monopoly game he made for New Year's Eve! He had taped down our pieces to keep them exactly where they were when I left to go to Michelle's party.

"I knew we'd finish the game one day," he said with his adorable smile.

I was so happy that I leaned across the table and gave him a big kiss . . . but one second later, my competitive nature took over and I rolled the dice while secretly tallying up how many Broadway shows I had to own to win. Our waiter let us stay and order numerous decaf lattes while we played, and after an hour and a half, I was finally declared the winner. Yay!

Since I'm in charge of making next year's New Year's Eve Monopoly game, I've already decided the theme will be our "favorite" teacher, E.R.! Every property will be an ailment she's had, like Hematoma Avenue and Staph Infection Place. And instead of "Go to Jail" cards, they'll say "Break a Hip." To win, you'll have to get the highest degree of whiplash.

Maybe Becky will help me make it on a Sunday afternoon. Oh yeah, since the dance, Becky, Spencer, and I have started a new tradition that on Sunday nights, the three of us rent a movie, and one of us is in charge of snacks. And Spencer and I invited her to spend New Year's Eve with us, too.

Back at school, a lot of the Cool U kids went back to ignoring me like they did before, but some are actually nicer. And a few of them have even started calling me to make plans. *And* so does Quincy.

Becky got into Usdan and we're both psyched to be spending the summer together, singing, dancing, and acting. Spencer's doing camp also, but his is a math camp (like I said before, every great guy has a tragic flaw). The good part is, it's a day camp like Usdan, so at least we'll get to see each other at night.

Summer vacation starts in three weeks. That means that sophomore year is almost over. Looking back, I'd say it was a combination of a little awesome and a lot awful. But the good news is, ever since I dumped my awful popularity plan, it's been only awesome.

I want to keep it this way, so I've made a vow to stop being like my parents: no more complicated plans and no more schemes.

That's right. No more manipulating situations to get what I want. I'm through with all of that.

Completely through.

Unless *absolutely* necessary . . .

A NOTE FROM SETH

HI, EVERYONE! THANKS FOR READING my very first young adult book. Although the story is totally made up, the character of Justin is similar to me. And not just in his nonstop fruitless search for pants that don't feel tight around the waist. I, too, had a hard time in school because I was made fun of for "acting gay," but thankfully I was able to make it to graduation without needing to concoct a popularity plan. If you're having a hard time because you think you might be gay or because kids make fun of you because *they* think you are, there is help! Go to TheTrevorProject.org or call 866-488-7386. And if you just need some reassurance that pretty much *everybody* had a horrible time in school, go to ItGetsBetter.org. You will not believe the number of amazingly cool, creative, and successful people who were considered complete losers when they were kids. Don't listen to the Doug Gools of the world!

If you want to email me, my website is sethrudetsky.com. Peace out, and hang in there!

ABOUT SETH

SETH RUDETSKY has been the afternoon Broadway host on SiriusXM radio since 2004. As a musician, he's played piano on Broadway for many shows (*Les Miz, Ragtime, Phantom*), and he music-directed the Grammy-nominated recording of *Hair* with Adam Pascal and Jennifer Hudson. As a TV actor, he's appeared on *Law and Order: Criminal Intent, Kathy Griffin: My Life on the D-List,* and MTV's *Made.* As a Broadway actor, he was in *The Ritz* with Rosie Perez and played opposite Sutton Foster in *They're Playing Our Song* in a fund-raiser for the Actors Fund. He writes a weekly column on Playbill.com and also wrote *The Q Guide to Broadway,* as well as *Broadway Nights,* of which there is an audiobook edition that features Seth, Kristin Chenoweth, and Jonathan Groff.

Seth lives in New York with his partner, James; his stepdaughter, Juli; and their two mutts, Sonora and Maggie. He loves reading young adult books; his favorites are *The Great Gilly Hopkins* by Katherine Paterson and the His Dark Materials trilogy by Philip Pullman.